Travelin' Money

At the end of a long cattle drive, Joe Sample runs into a little bad luck. A cantankerous steer pins him against a fence post, breaking his leg. So, Joe is laid up in the infamous Dog Stain Hotel next to Yuma pen. His money and the management's patience has run out when the door of the hotel restaurant bursts open and a wild-eyed man named Pierce Malloy walks in, his boot leaking blood. Malloy wants Joe to find a buried cache of money and give it to Tess Malloy whose husband has been hanged that morning. What choice does Joe have, being broke and about to be evicted?

He had accepted a little traveling money minutes before prison police arrive and gun Malloy down. With the money and a map to the treasure, Joe starts out to fulfil his promise to the dying man. Things do not turn out as planned however; the map leads him to a nest of thieves and an earthly hell.

Travelin' Money

Logan Winters

A Black Horse Western

ROBERT HALE · LONDON

© Logan Winters 2011
First published in Great Britain 2011

ISBN 978-0-7090-9255-1

Robert Hale Limited
Clerkenwell House
Clerkenwell Green
London EC1R 0HT

www.halebooks.com

Typeset by
Derek Doyle & Associates, Shaw Heath
Printed and bound in Great Britain by
CPI Antony Rowe, Chippenham and Eastbourne

ONE

It's rare to have someone help you out when you really need it. Especially if you happen to be down and out in the middle of a white-sand ocean without a spar to cling to. Which was where Joe Sample found himself. A rangy, sandy haired man who just now was forced to walk using a cane, not only was Joe broke, he was crippled and on the dark side of hope, sitting in the shadow of the gallows in a desert oasis called Dog Stain in Yuma, Arizona.

The gallows mentioned were very real. Just about every other day the hangman at Yuma prison took center stage at the noon hour and dropped the trap rehearsing for Sunday when the drop would be real beneath the feet of some condemned man or other. Joe Sample was used to the sound by now, but the first time he heard the grate and snap of the device it had jolted him out of his own self-pity and nearly caused him to spill his morning coffee on the floor of the Dog Stain Hotel.

The hotel had been built before there was a prison in Yuma, Arizona. A lady of dubious origin named Desiree Delfino had come there with her crusty man-friend, a desperado named Larkspur, or so Joe had been told, to build the most luxurious hotel in the territory – its name had originally been the Desiree-Royale – built to pave the way for Miss Delfino's grand entrance into Yuma's society, such as it was. The hotel was elegant, it was plush, with gilt fixtures on the walls and Arabian carpets on the floor, purchased with money the two pilgrims had made quickly somewhere and never wished to return to. The Royale was all Miss Delfino could have wanted. Until a mongrel dog sneaked into the main ballroom – as it was then called – and performed a natural, disgusting act on the sixteenth-century Persian carpet there the night of the Royale's grand opening.

Miss Delfino, witnessing this, flew into a rage which caused her to fall into an epileptic fit, Larkspur, in a way that could only have been expected of a highly indignant man of the West, began shooting at the scurrying perpetrator of the foul deed just as the local dignitaries began arriving. Larkspur shot the glass out of a window, wounded a city councilman and winged an impressive blue peacock imported for this special occasion.

Miss Delfino never recovered from the episode. The dignitaries fled before Larkspur's salvoes, and the Desiree-Royale surrendered to its inevitable decay, forced to accept the ignoble moniker it had borne forever afterwards: The Dog Stain Hotel.

Now it was butted up next to the white menace of the Yuma Territorial Prison, gutted of gilt and carpets, and surviving as cheap accommodation for penniless or near-penniless travelers, of which Joe Sample was one of the former.

Joe who had come to Yuma as a drover with a cattle herd owned by Poetry Givens with a gather of 300 Double Seven beeves meant to sustain the staff of the prison and the army garrison there, had gotten himself pinned up against a pole in the corral by a wild-eyed, half-ton brindle steer which did not know when to stop pushing, and awakened in bed at the Dog Stain with his leg broken in two places.

At first Joe Sample had enjoyed his rehabilitation at the Dog Stain. His upstairs room was one of pleasant decrepitude – unraveling carpet, faded wallpaper – but there was a high cathedral-type window from which he could gaze. Although the view was nothing but a few tumble-down adobes and a shack or two stretching out along the street in an easterly direction before the implacable desert resumed dominion, the sunrise was pretty through the smeared glass, and the bed, though a little noisy when he settled, was comfortable enough. It had everything over sleeping on the desert. But as the days, then weeks, passed by and his leg refused to heal properly, he got a little weary of the vista and squeaky bed, of staring at the faded, stained wallpaper.

At first Joe had enjoyed having kitchen-cooked meals, juicy steaks and homemade apple pie, followed by coffee and then a few beers at the adjacent saloon.

But after a while the money Poetry Givens had paid him off with ran out: 'Enough to see you through until your leg is better. You'll always have a job on the Double Seven, Joe,' was what Poetry had said at the time, and no doubt he had believed it. But the money was not enough. Eventually as his damaged leg continued to defy him, Joe had cut down on his food expenses, settling for biscuits and gravy for supper. The beer was now a luxury he could not afford. Joe spent most days at a table in the hotel restaurant sipping coffee, which he now had to request if he wanted his cup refilled, and this was done grudgingly by the help.

What was a broken-down cowboy to do when his game leg didn't allow for any travel?

Not so slowly, Joe Sample went broke. He had not a friend in Yuma, and the stable man had sold

Joe's horse to cover what he owed for its keep.

This was Joe Sample's condition when, that Sunday morning, hanging day at the prison, Pierce Malloy entered the restaurant, a wild look in his eye, his head swiveling as if searching frantically for assistance or unknown enemies. It was both, Joe discovered later. Malloy's eyes locked with those of Joe Sample and he walked heavily forward across the wooden floor toward Joe's table. Joe did not know Malloy except by name. The unusually well-dressed man had been in town for a week or so on private business and the two had nodded at intervals as they passed each other on the stairs or in the lobby.

Malloy approached Joe's table and sagged on to the wooden chair opposite. The usually impeccable man's black suit was dusty, his formerly waxed mustache fluffed out into untidy tufts of silver hairs. As he had crossed the room, Joe had noticed that Malloy was limping badly, more heavily than Joe himself, and there were spots of blood on his scuffed boots. That the leaking fluid seemed to be dripping from the top of the boot seemed to indicate that the entire boot was filled with blood. Malloy seated himself, placing his hands flat on the table to ease his change of position. Seated, he threw back his head, and breathed in heavily through his mouth. A shallow sigh emerged from his throat. Malley composed himself and thrust

9

out a hand.

'Joe Sample, isn't it?'

'Yes, sir,' Joe said, taking Malloy's hand which was pale, had long tapered fingers like a musician's but with an unusually strong grip.

'I thought I remembered,' Malloy said, sighing again. He touched his fingers to his heart and breathed in deeply, slowly, 'I'd like to offer you a proposition, Mr Sample.'

'Me?'

'I understand that you are down on your luck.'

'That's an understatement,' Joe answered. 'I'm close to the bone – can't pay for my hotel or board, can't buy a horse. . . .'

Malloy went on as if Joe had not spoken. 'There isn't much time,' Malloy said in a whispery voice. He looked back across his shoulder. 'I'll never make it out of Yuma, let alone back to Newberry Town. You see, I just shot the prison warden.'

As if to emphasize his confession, the trap of the gallows banged open as it was tested for the Sunday execution. Joe started a little. 'I don't see—' Joe began. Malloy cut him off.

'I'll be next,' Malloy said, glancing toward the window beyond which the gallows could be seen within the prison courtyard. 'I tried to do right but. . . . I understand you need some help, Joe. I can help you,' Malloy said, his eyes growing anxious, eager, 'if you will promise to help me.'

'If the law's after you, I can't get involved,' Joe replied, holding his hands up, palms toward Malloy.

'I don't want you to get into my fight. Nothing like that,' Malloy said, glancing toward the door behind him again. 'You see, I can't travel either. Not now. I think my shin bone's cracked.

'What I'm willing to do, Joe Sample, is to grub-stake you – I'm offering you a little traveling money if you will ride to Newberry and deliver something to the woman who's about to be widowed there.'

'Your wife?' Joe asked.

'Not mine.' Malloy glanced toward the gallows where a thin figure was being led up the steps. 'His! That's my brother, Amos. I thought I could get to the warden – he's been known to take a bribe – and work out a way that Amos could beat the noose. Amos has a new bride, pretty little thing and . . . but the warden wouldn't listen. It seems he took a particular dislike to Amos. Well, I lost my temper, he lost his.' Malloy nodded toward his leg. 'I've failed my brother, failed Tess.'

Malloy reached into his jacket pocket and withdrew a billfold. 'I want to give you this – a little traveling money, Joe, if you'll ride up there and tell Tess what has happened, and give her something my brother has hidden out for her. I won't lie to you – it's ill-gotten gains, but she will need it more

11

than the Territory of Arizona does. That's what I was going to offer to the warden if he'd let Amos off. . . .

'Take this, Joe,' Malloy said and he shoved four large banknotes and a small stack of gold money across the table. It was, Joe saw at a quick count, around $200. A fortune for someone in his situation.

'A little traveling money, you'll need it. I just want you to do this one favor for me. I'll draw you a map of where Amos left his package.' Malloy had produced an envelope and was hastily sketching on the back of it.

Joe said, 'You're talking about a stash of stolen money?'

'It was taken from someone who shouldn't have had it in the first place – it was Amos's money. I can't explain it all right now, Joe. There's little time. I just want you to do this for me, since I won't be able to do it myself.' Malloy slid the map across the table. Joe pocketed it hesitantly.

'How do you know you can trust me, Mr Malloy?' he asked, and Malloy answered thinly.

'I don't really have a lot of choice, Joe. Not now,' he added as the back door of the restaurant banged open. Six men burst in, two of them wearing prison guard uniforms.

One of them shouted out. 'Here he is!' and raised the rifle he was carrying. Malloy, quick as a

12

cat, drew his revolver and rolled to the floor, firing upward. He shot two of the pursuers, before they gunned him down, the bullets driving those present to seek cover behind the counter, under tables, as the acrid smoke roiled across the room.

One of the jailers nudged the inert body of Pierce Malloy with his boot toe. Another turned on Joe Sample, who was just rising from behind the table, bracing himself because of his gimpy leg. 'What part do you have in this?' the man in uniform demanded roughly.

Joe said truthfully: 'I don't even know the man. He wanted to sit in the first chair he came to. It was at my table.'

'Are you saying you aren't involved?' the guard demanded.

'I don't even know what I'm not involved in,' Joe answered with a poor attempt at a smile.

The members of the pursuing band watched with doubt and some impatience as the crippled cowhand picked up his cane from the floor and hobbled off toward his room. Joe heard one of them say, 'That man knows something,' and another answer:

'What's the difference now? We got Pierce Malloy, didn't we?'

That was that, Joe thought as he sat on his bed, the money Malloy had given him spread out on the sun-faded blue bedspread. Two hundred and

13

twenty dollars. A fortune. Enough riches to escape this trap he found himself in. Payment for a small favor. Transporting stolen treasure. . . . Joe Sample frowned as he pondered that. Pierce Malloy hadn't actually said that it was stolen, but that it was 'ill-gotten'. But Joe had gotten the idea.

What did it matter to him! If it was stolen, let the law take care of that. The money he had in front of him now had been freely given to perform a task. Deliver the package, the fortune – whatever it was – to a woman named Tess living in Newberry. Joe didn't know where the town was, but someone would know. There weren't that many self-sustaining towns in the desert.

If the 'treasure' was stolen, too bad for whoever it had come from. Joe only knew that he had taken money to deliver this 'package', and he had made his promise to a dying man. A vow like that has to be taken seriously.

It was too bad there hadn't been time to hear the whole story, but the prison guards had taken care of that. Joe would have liked to know where the money came from, why they had hanged Amos Malloy, what Pierce Malloy's role had been in acquiring the money, and who it was supposed to belong to.

For now, Joe Sample concentrated on his own business.

He threw his spare shirt and handful of other

worn clothes on to a blanket and rolled it tightly. After consideration, he left his cane behind. He would make it somehow.

Assuming a calm reserve he did not feel, Joe paid the panther-eyed man at the downstairs hotel desk. The clerk who had been eyeballing Joe hard during this last week now turned on the charm as money exchanged hands, and even told Joe that he valued his patronage.

Joe needed a horse – that was the first thing. Shouldering his bedroll, he walked out into the blinding light of the heated south Arizona day. Tugging his hat lower, he limped toward the stable where he had left and then lost his little sorrel pony. The shade cast by the stable interior did nothing to cool anyone on this sun-bright, desolate day when not a breath of wind blew. The inhabitants of Yuma were hiding out in their dwellings or in the saloons; not a dog wandered the streets. The local teamsters and laborers had started their work before dawn and were now finished for the day. The pale sky above the prison shimmered as if smoke were suspended there in the hundred-degree heat.

'What can I do for you? Oh, it's you. Look, mister, you hadn't paid for—' The narrow stableman had a truculent voice, fear in his siesta-blurred eyes. He glanced around as if for a weapon, remembering Joe's temper the last time the two had met. Joe's ire at finding that his little horse had been sold to a cash buyer had triggered his anger and frustration with events.

'Take it easy, Wolfe, I just came over here looking to buy another horse.'

'Oh, is that so? Sure, Mr Samples. What'd you do? Turn up the right card?'

'Something like that,' Joe said. He dropped his bedroll to the ground and drifted down the musty walkway between the stabled horses' stalls. Wolfe – a tall, gaunt man in striped gray coveralls and a torn straw hat – was nearly on his heels. Joe paused to stroke the muzzle of a fine-looking bay horse with lively eyes.

'That horse is stabled up here privately,' Wolfe said. 'Fact is, only the tall black down at the end and this little buckskin are for sale. The others are all owned.' Joe nodded, frowning. Too bad – he liked the spirited look of the bay.

Wolfe told him, 'I got other stock around back. I keep 'em outside. Those who pay for their horses' keep get the *de*-luxe accommodations. I'd be happy to show them other animals to you.'

The stableman led the way out into the brilliant, heated sunlight where a dozen or so horses could be seen crowded together in the scant shade of a lean-to constructed of unbarked poles and brush. Horseflies troubled them. Tails and ears twitched futilely trying to keep the insects away. There was only half a troughful of greenish, brackish water for the horses. Joe took a liking to two of the animals. There was a spry looking blue roan three or four years old, built for speed, and a dumpy wide-built buckskin with a black mane and tail that looked like it was a long-walking horse.

The young, prancing blue roan was tempting, but it seemed a little fragile for hard traveling, so eventually, after checking teeth and ligaments, eyes and hoofs, Joe decided on the buckskin. 'I will need tack,' Joe said as Wolfe led the buckskin out of the pen by its mane.

'I think I've got a saddle that'll suit.'

He did. It was Joe Sample's own old saddle. Apparently the new owner of his lost sorrel horse was more particular than Joe was. It grated a little, buying back his own saddle, but it wasn't Wolfe's fault that Joe hadn't paid him for keeping his horse.

Wolfe voluntarily saddled Joe's new horse for him in deference to Joe's injured leg and the cash money with which he had paid him. As the stable-man was tightening the twin cinches on his Texas-rigged saddle, Joe asked him:

'Did you ever hear of a place called Newberry?'

'Newberry?' Wolfe's long face creased with deep thought. 'I believe it's up toward Flagstaff, if it's the place I'm thinking of. Was it ever called Newberry Falls?'

17

'I wouldn't know.'

'I believe that's the place. The county recorder has maps of the entire territory – you might want to stop and ask him.'

'I probably will. Thanks,' Joe said, letting Wolfe give him a leg up into the saddle. He had spent hours, days, years perched on it, but it felt new and different after his long rehabilitation.

'Is that where you're headed?' Wolfe asked. 'Newberry?'

'I don't really know,' Joe said. 'I suppose I'll get there eventually.'

'Well, thanks,' the stableman said. 'I hope you have a safe trip. And I hope we'll be seeing you back in Yuma one day.'

Joe stifled a laugh. 'When the desert starts sprouting pomegranate trees.'

'Huh?'

'Thanks for the help, Wolfe,' Joe said, turning the buckskin horse's head toward the open twin doors at the front of the stable.

Joe rode the horse at an easy walk down the main street of town. He glanced at the mostly-illegible sign on the hotel face. Beneath the sun-blistering he could still make out the once-gilt lettering, 'Desiree Royale', faded and beaten as the lady who had built the place must be by now.

He went in to see the county recorder's maps and emerged in minutes. Wolfe had been right –

Newberry was in the direction of Flagstaff – a long, long way off. He stopped at the general store to purchase a few supplies from a fat, sun-reddened, almost hostile, desert-defeated woman, and started on his way again. He wondered if the storekeeper knew that she was better off now than the flamboyant Desiree Delfino.

Before taking his final leave of Yuma, Joe halted the buckskin horse in the scant shade of a lone cottonwood, its curling dry leaves stirring in the rising wind from the east. He withdrew the envelope with the treasure map Pierce Malloy had scrawled on its back, tried to orient himself, and then started on. He wasn't sure he could ever find the location Malloy had sketched, let alone deliver whatever it was to Amos Malloy's widowed bride. If there was blood on the money, so be it – that was something for the widow Malloy to carry on her conscience, not him.

With the sun still floating high in the sky, Joe started riding out on to the long desert – the whitest, emptiest, most desolate and cleanest country in the nation.

Leaving the Dog Stain behind.

TWO

'I'll have that horse! And before you move, I'm warning you that I shoot to kill.'

In the west a blue velvet dusk had settled above the mountains, the red half-eye of the sun gleaming through the gathering murk. The man who had yelled out to Joe Sample stood on a low, humped sand dune where a few determined strands of thorny briars had pushed through, searching for air and sustenance. Joe glanced toward the narrow figure; then turned back to his cooking. Behind him the lazy meandering creek he had been following northward was faintly audible.

He had started bacon frying, had beans from a tin can ready and pan bread dough mixed. The smoke from his mesquite wood fire curled lazily toward the darkening skies, its pleasant, raw scent mingling with that of the heating food.

'What are you, deaf?' the man with the rifle yelled out, his voice raspy, dry.

'I've got supper cooking,' Joe answered. 'It's the only meal I'll be having today, and I'm anxious to taste it. I've also got a pint pot of coffee. Why don't you come down and join me?'

'Why don't you just do as you're told!'

'You haven't told me to do anything yet, and I probably wouldn't do it anyway. If you shoot now, you'll ruin supper for both of us – and likely breakfast tomorrow. I know you've got me in your sights; I know you said you shoot to kill, but if it happens that you don't hit my vitals with your first shot, you'll note that I am wearing a gun, and if you give me a chance I'll be shooting back. I'm not the world's best shot, but you aren't that far away from me, stranger. I expect I could tag you, even from my back.'

Joe suggested: 'How about eating something first, then you can tell me what it is that's bothering you?'

The stranger shuffled down the sandy knoll. As he approached, Joe noticed defeat in the thin man's eyes. Another of life's explorers losing his way.

'Help yourself to a cup of coffee. It should be done by now.'

The thin man squatted on his heels and poured dark coffee from the small pot. He paid particular attention to the common utensils Joe had. 'All of your gear is brand new,' he commented, 'but you're no pilgrim.'

'I had to start over from nothing. I ran into some bad luck.'

'That is my horse,' the stranger said, pointing toward the buckskin Joe had purchased. He took a sip of coffee, raising his gaunt, firelit face to Joe. 'I got myself into a mess back in Yuma. The man across the table had three kings when I thought he was drawing to the flush showing. I lost my ready money and had to sell my horse or get kicked out of the hotel – Dog Stain – does that name mean anything to you?'

'I'm afraid it does,' Joe said, helping himself to a cup of coffee. Night birds were singing along the creek. Chatty, energetic chirps.

'I thought I could win my horse back if the right card turned. It didn't,' the stranger said morosely.

'That's why I'm not a gambler,' Joe said. 'There's only two things that can happen and I don't like one of them.'

'Losing.' The man's head nodded. He stroked his fingers down the stringy flesh of his throat 'You'd think a man would learn better as he got older.'

'Oh, we learn better,' Joe said with a short laugh, 'it just doesn't stop us from doing it.'

'I guess that's it,' the stranger said. 'What is it

that happened to you, Mr. . . ?'

'My name's Joe Sample,' Joe said extending a hand.

'Tittle Sparks,' the man at the fireside answered. Joe reached in to keep the beans from burning and slapped a few spoonfuls on to each of the tin plates he had taken from his pack. Why he had even purchased two he could not have said. But now and then a man does run across a companion even in the wildest places – if Tittle Sparks, rifle in hand, could be considered a companion. Still, if a hungry man came looking for a meal, you never refused him – not out here.

'You were going to tell me how you lost your poke,' Sparks said.

'It wasn't exactly like that,' Joe replied, and he began telling Sparks the story of having his leg broken by a steer in the holding pen. It wasn't really much of a story, he realized, but Sparks was riled by it.

'And your boss, this Poetry Givens, you mean he just left you behind in Yuma?' Darkness was settling; the firelight deepened the creases in Spark's face.

'He paid me off – I don't know what else he could have done.'

'I think I've heard of the man,' Sparks said, greedily shoveling the last of the pan bread into his face after sopping up the bean juice with it.

23

'The Double Seven is down toward Alamogordo, isn't it?'

'Socorro,' Joe corrected.

Sparks went on with some heat in his words. 'I know that ranch. They say that Givens named it the Double Seven because then his smith would only have to make that one iron – "7" – this way, then it could turned upside down to burn another "7" the other way.' Sparks sketched the Z-like Double Seven brand in the earth. 'Isn't that what it looks like?'

'Yes, sevens butt to butt.' Joe was puzzled. What was the man getting at?

'Because it was the cheapest way to design the brand!' Sparks said with triumphant confidence. 'It saved iron.'

'Well, I doubt—'

'So that's the man who left you down and out in Yuma! It figures.'

'My leg just took longer to heal than anyone would have guessed.'

'Now you don't have a job, is that it? Now that you're crippled, Poetry has no use for you.'

'Poetry's not like that – he has a couple of yardmen on the ranch who got themselves hobbled up years ago. He takes care of them well enough.'

'But they get paid less, I'll wager.'

Joe was tired of discussing the character of Poetry

Givens. He had always been treated well by the ranch owner. 'It wasn't Poetry's fault,' Joe insisted. 'As for taking care of me – he's not my daddy. I get paid for looping steers. I do my job; he pays me. That's reasonable. The only way this could have been avoided was if I was clever enough never to become a cowboy.'

'If you say so,' Sparks muttered. 'Anyway, I guess it all worked out for you. Seeing all this new camp gear you have tells me that something turned up for you. So I guess,' he acknowledged grudgingly, 'that you aren't a thief, that you had enough money to buy my horse from that lowlife, Wolfe, down in Yuma.'

'Do you want to see the bill of sale?' Joe offered, reaching into his pocket.

'No,' Sparks answered, waving him off. 'I suppose I was just a little touchy. Having no food in my belly, no water, no place to go and no way to get here.'

'A man can get desperate,' Joe agreed. 'Just don't let it lead you to shooting solutions.'

'Well, son, I was ready to start grazing on sand,' Sparks said, leaning forward, his hands on the knobs of his bony knees. 'I suppose I should be thanking you for that meal instead of complaining to you. But it's hard times for sure.' After a thoughtful minute as the last light of the dying sun faded from the blue sapphire sky, he asked:

'Where are you headed, Joe?'

'Eventually to the Double Seven,' Joe said hesitantly. Poetry told me I'd always have a job there. But there's a few stops I have to make along the way.'

'Where's that?' Sparks asked, leaning forward, squinting narrowly at Joe.

'I'll be needing to stop for a few more supplies,' Joe answered vaguely.

'Seems to me you're pretty well stocked,' Sparks said, nodding at the burlap bags that held Joe's provisions.

'Think so?' Joe said warily. Sparks seemed too interested in his material goods. No matter – it had been a long day and the evening was cool; Joe decided to curl up in his blanket with the last flickering red and gold remnants of his fire lighting the dark camp.

But he chose to sleep with his Colt revolver in his hand.

Dawn was a scarlet blur across the eastern horizon. Joe awoke stiff and lightly coated with sand. He sat up, clenched his knees and groaned, and looked around for Tittle Sparks. The long-faced, narrow built man was gone. As was the buckskin horse. And his saddle-bags containing his traveling money.

Too angry with himself to rise and curse the

skies or chase after the man, Joe sat, thinking about how stupidly trusting a man can be. Sparks had announced his intention to take the horse, had nearly flat-out said that he was there to rob Joe whom he took to be a wealthier man than he, and yet Joe had let it happen.

Joe Sample had never considered himself overly-bright, but the episode was a new low in wisdom, even for him. Thinking about it, he considered that a part of his trusting nature came from having worked in an environment on the Double Seven, where, as on almost all ranches, a man could depend on his partners – simply because he had to. On the range if you could not depend on a man to bring help when it was needed – on an occasion when some ornery bronc might toss you or a snake bite you – well, you just had no one to count on.

Which explained why so many cowboys ending a cattle drive caused such a huge ruckus in trail-head towns – places they would never be invited back again. Months on the trail forged bonds. Fighting weather, Indians and half-wild animals brought the crews closer together than any army. One man might get into a dispute in one of those towns, be it Abilene or Wichita, any place you care to name, and his brothers of the saddle naturally came to his aid until things got too far out of hand. The ranch bosses didn't like it, but they understood it and knew they needed that sort of unity among their men. They would grudgingly pay off any fines and lay into the cowboys, meaning only half of it, then return to the home ranch.

That was the way it was. But Joe was just a little too old to be as gullible as he seemed to have become, trusting his fellow man. Still grumbling as he surveyed the empty white-sand desert around him, Joe recalled that Sparks hadn't even had a kind word to say about Poetry Givens who was the best boss Joe had ever hired out to.

'Well, damn you, Tittle Sparks,' he swore. 'I've never met a man low enough to take supper at my fire and steal my pony in the night, leaving me afoot in country like this!'

He knew he wasn't going to strike out across the flats. The Double Seven outfit had just finished driving a herd across that land beneath a white sun. Most of the cattle had made it, but there were a lot of bones and hides scattered out there. He made his way back toward the creek he had been following. Not knowing the area, even the name of the slow-moving, green-water stream, he was uncertain where it would lead. But any water in this wasteland offered a promise of life, and if there was a small ranch or community out this way, it would most likely abut the stream.

Joe took a breath and trudged forward. The high sandy banks of the creek were clotted with willow brush, nopal cactus and little else. The morning was tolerable enough as the bank to the east provided him with shade while he tramped along, shuffling over twigs, cactus and rocks, but when the sun reached its noonday azimuth, the heat of it fell like an iron brand across his shoulders and back.

He had water – he was grateful for that. Without it he would not have lasted a day. What his shrinking stomach urged him to do was to find some source of nourishment but nothing offered itself up to his hopeful searching. There were fish in the stream – bluegills, he thought – although he never got close enough to the darting silver fish to be sure. He had no line, nothing to forge a hook out of, and his one attempt at using a length of sharpened wood to spear one proved only embarrassing. He shuffled forward, following the stream hopefully.

He found nothing to eat, not a cottontail rabbit, not a rattlesnake – although by the signs in the sand, they were plentiful enough. And there was no shade! He could have crossed the creek to the other side where shadows would be falling sooner, but that would slow him down and likely ruin his boots.

Cursing Tittle Sparks and the evil ways of men, he sat in mid-afternoon on a rock abutting the stream and soaked his bare feet in the flowing water. Cicadas buzzed in the underbrush and peeper frogs chorused in the dry reeds. Once a small covey of quail wandered past, glanced his way and fled on foot. It took a lot to startle them enough to take to wing.; they were hardly six-gun game. Beyond that and the constant pestering of gnats, nothing moved along the valley, and there was no sign that anything – man or horse – had done so for a long while.

Joe rubbed his sore feet and looked into his boot, seeing the two ten-dollar gold pieces. All that Sparks had left him to survive on. Not that they did Joe a bit of good out here where there was nothing to be purchased and no one to buy it from, which, he thought, showed you how valuable money was at the bottom.

But that cash might prove valuable when he did manage to reach some settlement – if such there were out here – and he offered silent thanks to old Foghorn Blaine, a stubby, whiskered old-timer who had once seen Joe starting toward town to spend his pay and celebrate a successful drive and told him with heartfelt remonstrance: 'Son, you have to always keep something to boot. You never know when you might need it.'

And when it won't do you any good at all to have it, Joe was thinking, but Foghorn had been right – even having an extra dollar or two set aside could sometimes save a man from having to live like a crawling mongrel dog. People are apt to help you more if you can show them a little silver or a piece of gold – that's just the way things are.

It was coming on to purple twilight when Joe saw the lights shining in the distance. The banks of the river had flattened, and looking toward the east, he could see the shimmering lights of what appeared to be a small town. He could hardly choke back the cry of relief in his throat as he struggled up the sandy bluff to solid, flat ground on blistered feet. He stood as a man amazed before he began plodding on toward the hopeful sign of civilization.

Joe wanted a horse more than anything in this world. No, he wanted food for his shrunken stomach. He wanted to find Sparks and teach that man a real lesson about respect. Or, more than anything, he realized, as he staggered toward the distant lights, he wanted to see another human face, talk to someone, anyone at all. . . .

The first person he met was not the one Joe would have chosen.

'Well, ain't you a belly-crawler!'

'I don't know,' Joe said hoisting his hands since the pudgy man standing before him in the near-darkness had a shotgun leveled at him. 'I'm not familiar with the term.'

'You ain't?' the hard-boiled man said, not lowering his shotgun an inch. 'That's what we call those like you who come dragging in off the desert. Half of 'em's army deserters, others broke-down prospectors who lost their burro to a rattlesnake. Now and then we even get somebody who's broke out of Yuma Prison – murderers and bank robbers and such. Which kind are you, stranger?' he demanded of Joe.

'None of those,' Joe shrugged. Behind the man was the rough shape of a poorly made house. The sky at sunset was milky blue, a flare of reddish light sketched across it. The shallow creek behind him still announced itself with trickling sounds. The air was scented with a familiar, unappetizing barnyard smell.

The man with the shotgun continued to scowl at Joe, wanting an explanation from this 'belly-crawler'.

'Someone took my horse and gear and left me out on the desert,' Joe said.

'Friend of yours?'

'Not much,' Joe said with a weak smile.

'You should have been more careful.'

'I guess I should have,' Joe agreed.

'Where was you heading?' the armed man asked with a hint of slyness, as if he were trying to outwit Joe.

'Newberry – do you know where that is?'

'Is that where you come from?' the man with the shotgun asked, ignoring the question. 'Up that way?'

'No, I'm from Socorro, actually. It's kind of a long story, friend. Do you mind us talking about it without that gun in my face?'

'No, we are pretty friendly around Pierce Point.'

'Is that what this place is called?' Joe asked.

'Of course it is.' The man looked pityingly at Joe. 'Man, you don't know where you are or where you're going, do you?'

'That about covers it,' Joe was forced to admit. 'Any chance of a man getting something to eat? It's been a long time since I've put my teeth to any meaningful work.'

'That depends – have you got any money with you?'

'A little,' he answered. There was a little silver money in his jeans that Sparks hadn't been able to get at, plus his boot money, which he resolved not to show to anyone for the time being.

'All right,' the man with the shotgun growled, 'come up to the house. Addie will make you something – for a price.'

The breeze stirred as Joe followed the bulky figure of the man along a narrow path winding between thick stands of nopal cactus and scattered creosote bushes; the breeze did nothing to cool the skin, but it lifted scattered light debris – chiefly chicken feathers, which explained the scent of the place. To one side Joe noticed a long, squat, lath structure, and from it emanated fluttering, com-

33

plaining, squawking noises indicating that the hens had not yet settled for the night and were having a hard time doing so. Finally they reached the house in the near darkness.

'Mind your boots,' the gun-toting stranger told Joe as he stepped on to the rear porch to the house. 'Addie is not fond of chicken-droppings on her floor.'

Joe scraped his boots on the iron scraper fastened to the planks of the porch and walked hesitantly into the house.

It was unexpectedly, comfortably, cool inside the small house although a fire was burning in the iron stove of the kitchen. A sturdy, amiable-looking woman with graying hair and only a comfortable padding of weight on her tall frame stood in one corner, arms folded over her aproned figure.

'Wipe your boots, Mose?' she asked Joe's escort.

'Yes'm,' Mose answered like a dutiful boy. 'This here belly-crawler wishes for something to eat. He says he has money to pay for it.' Seen in the light, Mose's appearance was even more imposing. His face looked as if it had been pushed in and somehow managed to unfold itself again. Bashed, flat nose and sagging, rugged jaw. When he smiled, Joe saw half a dozen yellow stumps of what had once been teeth.

Across the room at a rough plank table sat another man. He was lanky, with a sparse black beard he had not given to a razor in a while. His eyes were morose, his face sullen, jaw set with some sort of dark expectation. He, too, had a long gun – a Winchester rifle – placed on the table before him.

Joe was beginning to feel more ill at ease as the younger man's hand began working its way along the weapon's stock as if he wanted to reach the action.

The woman, Addie, waved a cautioning hand at the younger man and warned him: 'You just sit still, Solomon! There's time enough for killing this here belly-crawler after he's eaten.'

THREE

Moses and Solomon had trooped away into the interior of the house, muttering something in undertones about needing a drink. Addie chuckled cheerfully as she approached Joe, her arms still folded across her breast.

'Don't tell me that you took me seriously about killing you, stranger! That's just my way of joking. Moses and Solomon seem always ready to go off half-cocked when they see a man they haven't met before. It comes from living out here on the fringe of the world for so long. I have to remind them to watch their manners.'

'I see,' Joe answered, sagging on to a bench behind the kitchen table. No, he did not see the humor in it. His eyes constantly flitted to the doorway where Moses and Solomon had gone to get liquored-up – and then?

'Mose says you might have a nickel or two to pay

for some food,' Addie said in a businesslike way.

'Whatever you can offer,' Joe said.

'It's more a matter of what you can offer,' Addie said.

Joe dug into his sun-faded jeans and brought out what was nearly a dollar in silver – a quarter-dollar, a few dimes, a couple of nickels. 'Will that do for a meal?' Joe asked.

'A few slices of bread,' Addie replied, wasting no time in swiping the change from the table, 'and some *huevos con huevos.*'

'What's that? I don't get you,' Joe told her.

'This close to the Mexican border and you don't even speak any kitchen Spanish?' Addie said, going to a cupboard to reach for a pot and a few dishes.

'No, I don't.'

'I'll bet you know a few words of love,' Addie said, lowering her heavy eyelids coyly.

'Not even those.'

'Ah, I wonder, then, what sort of man you are!' Addie exclaimed.

'That's long been a puzzle to a lot of people,' Joe said with a narrow smile. Addie laughed.

'Well, then, stranger. When I spoke, I meant that this is an egg ranch, if you haven't noticed by the smell – we make a few dollars selling them in town. What I offered you is eggs and eggs – it's about all we have.'

'How about fried chicken?' Joe suggested hopefully.

'Only for Sunday dinner,' Addie responded. 'And then you'd have to fight Mose and Sol to come up with so much as a wing or the part that goes over the fence last.'

'I don't think I'd care to try that.'

'No,' Addie said, 'you wouldn't. But don't let it be said that Adelaide Comfort can't fry an egg. Take off your hat and unbelt your gun and I'll fix you up, stranger.'

'Joe,' he told her. 'My name is Joe Sample.' He placed his worn hat aside. 'If it's not impertinent, I believe I'll keep my Colt where it's riding.'

Addie glanced toward the door where the men had gone and told Joe, 'They don't mean nothing, not really, but they fool a lot of people into thinking they do.'

And I'm one of them, Joe thought, but did not say. He had already made up his mind he would eat what he was served and flee at the first opportunity. There was a town nearby – Pierce Point – and with the forty dollars in his boot he could probably find some sort of nag to carry him along on this odyssey, which was beginning to feel less like a debt of honor than a misguided quest.

After all, what did he owe Pierce Malloy or his hanged brother, Amos? He had a brief blurry vision of a young widow crying for her husband, waiting for a few dollars to keep her from destitution, but Joe rubbed that away with the heels of his hands as Adelaide Comfort served his buttered toast and eggs.

What did he owe Pierce Malloy? Nothing – but he had given his word, and when a man has given that, he has pledged his bond more strongly than any court or law can enforce, if he were to remain a man.

Well, he had not yet even found the treasure he was supposed to deliver to Tess Malloy and probably never would.

When he had finished eating; Joe asked 'Any chance of getting shelter for the night?'

'Got another twenty-five cents?' the practical Adelaide asked.

'I think I can manage that.'

'Well, then,' she said, glancing toward the door beyond which the men had begun making some sort of drunken racket, 'we can put you up. Out in the tool shack where Dub stays.'

'Dub?'

'You'll meet him. He's harmless, if a little loose in the head. Let me see that silver,' she demanded and pocketed it in her apron, apparently to keep it out of the sight of Moses and Solomon, knowing what they would spend it on.

Joe cared less about Dub being a little loose in the head than he did about spending a night anywhere near Moses and Solomon. These both seemed unstable and quick to go to guns. The obvious poverty of the chicken farm made Joe sure that these two would have no problem rousting him for the forty gold dollars he had remaining.

Adelaide Comfort did not escort Joe out into the dark of night; but only opened the back door and pointed at a ramshackle building near the chicken barn. Joe stepped out into the night and the door was closed sharply behind him. He paused, thinking he would be better off walking to the town of Pierce Point, not far distant by the lights he saw, but he was very tired, his feet blistered and swollen, and what sort of brigands and bullies would he wander into in Pierce Point? Spending a night with Dub could not be that bad – Joe still had his Colt if the man was more than a little loose in the head.

Joe crossed the chicken-smelling yard in the darkness, and found the shack. Rapping on the flimsy door he entered without waiting for a response. A narrow young man was stretched out on a cot, starlight illuminating his eyes.

'Dub?' Joe inquired.

'Yes, sir,' a dubious voice answered.

'My name's Joe. Addie told me I can spend the night over here.'

'What Addie says is the rule,' Dub said, sitting up in bed. He wore a white long john shirt and faded

40

blue jeans. He stretched once and yawned. 'Addie's the chicken boss; me, I'm just the wrangler.' Dub smiled as if he had thought up that joke a long time ago and had been waiting for the time to come when he could spring it on someone. It was a weak affair, but Joe smiled in the darkness.

'There's a cot – you'll have to open it. Came from an old army camp,' Dub said.

As Joe's eyes adjusted to the poor light he saw that Dub had one folded ear like a mongrel dog, and a nose which wandered from one side of his face to the other. He was smiling broadly, but it seemed to Joe that this was not out of humor, but because his lips did not cover his gapped, bucktoothed ivory. His hair was probably reddish-brown, but it was difficult to make out color in that poor light.

Dub was on his feet, helping Joe with the unfolding of the canvas cot's wooden legs. He was inches taller than Joe, only half as thick through the torso. One suspender drooped down from his shoulder. When he spoke again, it was with concern.

'You don't have no money, do you?'

'Me?' Joe laughed. 'Not to speak of.'

'I only ask because Sol and Mose will surely come after it.' Dub's eyes flitted around the shack. 'I wouldn't want to be here if they come out drunk and ready to shoot.'

'They scare you, do they?'

'Yes, that's so. And they've scared a few other men in their time.'

'I can see how they might.'

Dub said chillingly, 'A few of them that they've scared are buried around here – still scared.'

'But they don't bother you?' Joe asked, sitting on the bare cot. Dub tossed him a blanket – obviously army-issue as well.

'Not me,' Dub told him, sitting on his own cot facing Joe in the moody shadows of the night. 'I ain't got no money. But they bothered them soldiers – they did have some of their pay.'

Joe liked nothing about the way this was tending. He reconsidered going into Pierce Point and shook off the notion. If the two had meant to assault him, they would have already done so. Besides, he still had his Colt and was not deeply afraid of two drunken chicken farmers.

He asked Dub, 'Do you know this area well?'

'I can make my way around.'

'Do you know Newberry?'

'Sure – used to be called Newberry Springs. Up in the dry hills maybe twenty miles north.'

'How about . . .' Joe hesitated about doing it, but he was not likely to get anywhere on his own. He removed the folded envelope with its scrawled map from his shirt pocket and leaned forward, asking Dub, 'Would you have an idea where this might be?'

Dub leaned forward studying the map earnestly. Joe thumbed a match to life to provide some illumination, which agitated Dub.

'Don't light no fire – it disturbs the chickens and they can't roost!'

'I doubt this light . . .' Joe snuffed out the match. There was no point in arguing with the kid when he needed his help.

'Is this Mustang Ridge?' Dub asked. In the darkness Joe could not see what Dub was indicating. ' 'Cause if it is, this is Candlewick Creek and the old oak grove up there.'

'How far is that?' Joe asked.

'On the way to Newberry – something like fifteen miles,' Dub answered.

That must be the place then. The trouble was, Joe had no horse, no supplies and did not know the area. Nor anyone he could trust to guide him. Dub looked up and his lopsided smile broadened. He looked toward the door of the shack and said in a lisp:

'Here they come. Mose and Sol have decided to get after you, mister.'

Why, Joe did not know. Perhaps they had seen some of the silver he had given to Adelaide and figured he might have more. Possibly they had simply decided that they did not like him. Maybe they were just drunk out of their skulls and in need

43

of recreation. Why, did not matter at the moment. Their heavy boots could be heard rushing toward the shack. Dub gawked at the door, frozen into immobility.

The men crossed the flimsy porch and the door was banged open. Mose was the first one through. He had his shotgun in his hands. At the sight of the red-faced man, Dub let out a little yelp and darted for the door. As he brushed past Mose, Mose spun and tried to deliver a booted kick to Dub's rump.

Joe took his chance. He had never been a skilled fighting man, but he had learned a few things from the rough sort down on the Double Seven. One of these was that although a kick is probably the most effective blow a man can deliver, it also leaves him vulnerable. A man on one foot has no natural balance, no way of bracing himself as he follows through with it.

Joe made his rush. Before Moses had finished his kick, Joe plowed into him, spinning Mose around and knocking him through the door. The collision brought the two of them crashing to the swayed porch, Joe on top of Mose. The big man's head cracked against the planks. His eyes rolled back, and half out of fear that he might rise with that shotgun, Joe took to his heels, rushing away blindly past Solomon who seemed to be almost blind drunk and could only raise a weak cry of warning before Joe was past him, circling toward the lath hen house.

Solomon gathered his wits enough to fire a blast from his rifle which penetrated the insubstantial structure, setting off a flurry and flutter and squawk inside as the roosting hens were startled awake, and sent Joe diving toward the ground.

Joe turned and fired off-handedly at Solomon just to keep him away. The shot could have hit nothing, but Solomon yowled out a protest. The back door of the house was flung open and an angry Adelaide Comfort appeared there.

'Hey, you fools! Think those hens are going to lay after this ruckus?' She added a few unladylike curses as Joe got to his feet and slipped away into the darkness.

'Psst!'

It was Dub, appearing astride a mangy-looking red horse with wild eyes. 'Get aboard,' he said excitedly. '1 think we're both done with this chicken farm!'

It took half an hour to reach the small town of Pierce Point. They must have looked a sight. Two men on a weary old mare, unsaddled, since Dub had not had time to catch up any gear for the animal. The few looks they got from loungers along the street were more than a little curious.

'Find a place where we can swing down,' Joe

panted into Dub's ear. The old mare's spine was already rubbing his tailbone raw.

'Where?' Dub asked dully.

'It doesn't matter. A stable, I suppose. Maybe I can make a deal for a horse.'

'You got money?' Dub asked in surprise.

'Very damned little,' Joe said. His boot money. Forty dollars. Certainly not enough to lose his life over, if that was what Moses and Solomon had intended. 'I need to look at that map I showed you again, have you tell me which direction I need to take.'

'Sure,' Dub said. 'I'll even ride along with you if you'll have me.' He smiled, but without humor. 'I don't think I'll be going back to the egg ranch any time soon.'

'No,' Joe agreed, 'I don't suppose so – we'll talk it over.'

'But then maybe I should,' Dub said forlornly. 'It's fly season and I should have sprayed around the coops. Miss Addie gets awful peeved if those flies get up. And there's nothin' flies like better than warm chicken. . . .'

Exasperated, Joe flared up. 'Do what you like, Dub! Let me slip off the horse, and you ride on back there – do whatever you want to do.'

'I expect Miss Addie will put Mose and Sol to work doing that,' Dub said, his slow mind turning over again.

'I expect – find a stable, Dub.'

'I know where there's one,' Dub said brightly.

'Then put us there,' Joe said, his mood still stormy. He was wondering if the whole bunch of them at the chicken ranch – whatever their relationship was – didn't share some mental deficiency.

There was still enough light shining for Joe to make out a hand-painted sign decorating a tall building with open doors.

'Here's a stable,' he said to Dub.

'I don't know. Mose, he don't like the man in there.'

Joe was far beyond caring what Moses thought about the man – whoever he was. 'Draw up the mare or I'm kicking off,' he said to Dub.

'You're still awful antsy,' Dub complained, halting the red mare.

'Why – just because there's two armed men back there who tried to kill me earlier?'

'Maybe they were just funnin',' Dub speculated. 'They do that all the time.'

'Not to me,' Joe growled. 'I'm going in here, are you coming?'

'Mose, he always said that this. . . .' Dub began, and Joe slipped from the back of the bony red mare and walked into the stable, rubbing himself where it ached.

'Anybody here!' Joe called out into the horse-smelling darkness of the high-roofed stable. 'I need a little help!'

The fat man who came forward from the murkiness, hitching his pants up, was no more than five and a half feet high. His nose was bulbous and a pair of bulging eyes stared out around it.

'Well, what is it?' he said in a tone of complaint, scratching his enormous belly and squinting popeyed at Joe.

'Business,' Joe said, as he looked across his shoulder to see Dub entering timidly with the red mare in tow.

'Beg your pardon, mister.' the stable man said, 'but you don't look like you and me can do much business.'

'I don't mean to do much,' Joe answered. 'What I'm looking for is a good ten-dollar horse.' The man laughed, 'Is there such a thing!'

'I don't know. That's why I'm asking you.'

The stable man rubbed his florid cheeks. His eyes brightened momentarily. 'You aren't planning on going panning, are you? I got a donkey outside I purchased from a worn-down prospector. . . .'

'I don't appreciate being made fun of,' Joe said. 'Look here, have you got a decent *twenty*-dollar horse?'

Joe caught a glimpse of Dub's face, lighted with astonishment, and he thought that maybe the poor-living man had never seen so much money together in his life.

'I've got a dun, a 14-year-old gelding that can take a man from here to there. But I'd have to ask twenty-five for it.'

There was no point in haggling. Joe said, 'Let me have a look at him, then write me some paper – I don't wish to be taken for a horse thief.'

Again.

The stableman who had easily won their brief duel agreed readily and as Joe performed the most perfunctory check of the old animal's condition, and announced himself satisfied, the stable man scribbled out a bill of sale and signed it with a flourish.

'Do I get tack with that?' Joe asked as he slipped off his boot and handed over two gold pieces, which again caused Dub's eyes to light up.

'Generally a man has his own saddle,' the stable boss said, fishing the silver change out of a shallow green metal cash box.

'These aren't general times,' Joe responded, knowing that he was about to be gouged again. Just then he did not care. He wanted to be out of Pierce Point and on his way to Newberry if he could find it. Once that task was completed, maybe he could return to the Double Seven and get back to his peaceful life as a ranch-hand where all he would have to watch out for were the longhorn steers, rattlesnakes and the occasional puma.

49

They were much easier to deal with than men.

As the dun was saddled for him, he silently cursed the deceased Pierce Malloy for dragging him into this – and himself for having given his promise to do it.

But he did not forget that there was a worrying, heartbroken widow named Tess Malloy who was distraught, destitute and might possibly be at least a little comforted by the return of the 'ill-gotten' fortune Pierce Malloy had told Joe about.

It was a hard land for women, a hard one for young widows, even harder for one without resources.

With the purchase of the dun, which seemed surprised to find itself saddled and ridden again at its age when it probably thought retirement had finally arrived, Joe made only one more stop in Pierce Point. He found a general store, still open on this evening and forked over five dollars for basic trail supplies – flour, salt, bacon and beans. Along with these he purchased a spade. It would do. It would have to.

Then, ill-equipped, ill-mounted and ill-tempered, he led the way out on to the open desert with Dub plodding after him on the red mare.

FOUR

In the chill of the settling night they made their camp. Saguaro cactuses stretched long bristling arms skyward. The chalice of the night was cobalt blue, bright with stars that were like chips of ice. They had made their way only a few miles from the white desert flats up into the folded chocolate-colored hills, but the air was frigid as Joe and Dub rolled up in their blankets to pass an uncomfort-able night on the rocky ground.

'How far is this place we're looking for?' Dub stuttered, his teeth chattering with the cold.

'You said only another five miles or so,' Joe had to remind his reluctant guide.

'I guess I did,' the miserable Dub said. 'I guess I forgot. I've been worried about those chicken flies!'

'I told you that you could go back there if you want,' Joe said, gathering his blankets more tightly around him.

'I believe Mose would beat me. Probably Sol too, if he was inclined.'

'Couldn't Miss Adelaide stop that from happening?' Joe asked around a yawn. Truthfully he was already tired of his traveling companion and the problems on the chicken ranch.

'S-sometimes Miss Addie can, sometimes she can't. Mister Moses, he'll kick me when she's not looking. That hurts awful bad.'

'I understand. Look, I've still got a few dollars. After we find what I'm looking for you can take the money and go home, if you like.'

'I should never have. . . .' Dub started the sentence but fell asleep before he could continue. Joe knew what he was thinking, what he was going to say. The poor misfit had left the only home he had known, a poor one to be sure where he was abused. But where else could a half-bright kid like Dub hope to find work or a better life?

Well, tomorrow, when he hoped to come upon the 'treasure' site on the spot Pierce Malloy had indicated on his crudely-drawn map, Joe intended to indeed give Dub the last of his silver money and let the kid ride to whatever fate he had in store for him. He was not willing to adopt the pup.

Joe had his own task ahead of him. Take whatever there was to be found on the site, deliver it to Tess Malloy and go on about his own business which was simply trying to make the tired old dun horse deliver him across the hundreds of miles to Socorro and the safety of the Double Seven Ranch. He had never thought of the crowded smoky bunkhouse there as being a comfortable haven, but just now Joe was thinking that living there with the cook boiling coffee and frying bacon while his rowdy bunkmates cursed, scratched, joked and stamped their boots on as they rose was the most pleasurable of times. A steady job, steady friends. . . .

He himself fell to sleep despite the bitter cold.

Joe awoke with a hunger-inspired memory of the smell of the cinnamon buns Alicia Morales baked on certain mornings, thoughts of butter melting slowly on their oven-crisp tops. He sat up sharply, actually reaching down to clutch his stomach. Lord, he was starting to miss the old Double Seven. For all of the hard toil and rough men around him, it seemed like heaven in retrospect. He rubbed his head, stood, stretched and reached for his coffee pot, the second he had purchased in a week. He scraped together some branches from beneath the scrawny piñon pines that clung to the ledges surrounding their campsite, looked wonderingly at the long, rugged land beyond where ridges and hills folded together, collapsed on to each other, suddenly parted and widened into chasm-like canyons without reason or an apparent pattern. He hoped that Dub knew his way through this wild country.

Looking at poor Dub, still asleep in the cool of morning, Joe felt a small pang of regret, a little sense of superiority. If he could envision himself riding back on to Double Seven range, what was there for Dub to look forward to? He hadn't even the humiliating life he had led on the chicken ranch to return to.

To start the small fire necessary to boil coffee, Joe rolled the branches in his rough palms to separate the bark from them. Slowly, as the bark caught fire he added twigs to the flames. An unexpected breeze began to build, stuttering its way through the rocky hills.

When the fire had advanced from a flickering hope to a glowing entity, Joe walked to Dub's bed and tapped the toe of his own boot to the heel of Dub's worn brogues. Dub's eyes opened cautiously, one at a time, as if fearful of what the new morning might bring.

'Everything's all right,' Joe said, trying to sound cheerful. 'I've started some coffee boiling. I think we'll have to skip any idea of breakfast this morning.'

'No eggs?' Dub said, sitting up to gaze helplessly at Joe. His reddish hair hung over his forehead.

'I'm afraid not. We haven't any.'

'Addie always serves eggs.'

Joe sighed inwardly. Dub had previously been in the only place he had ever belonged despite the abuse he seemed to have taken from Moses and Solomon. Eggs to eat and a cot to sleep on were all he needed. Again Joe wondered if he was doing the kid a favor by taking him away from the egg farm, but that had never been his intention in the first place.

'Get up and have some coffee. Get your eyes open. I need to find that place on the map today.'

'You mean where the pirate treasure is?' Dub said, growing eager.

'That's right,' Joe said wearily. Dub had the wisdom and understanding of a 6-year-old. 'But it isn't mine. I have to take it to its rightful owner.'

'The pretty lady?'

'I don't know if she is pretty or not,' Joe answered, although Pierce Malloy had described Tess in those words. 'It doesn't matter. She needs it because her husband has died.'

'Out at sea, I know,' Dub said, lost in his own fantasy. He made his way to the low-smoldering camp-fire, scratching himself as he adjusted his suspenders, and shivered in the light, cool wind. Joe, squatting on his heels, poured each of them a cup of the boiled black coffee.

'Mose always puts whiskey in his coffee,' Dub said.

'Well, that's another thing we don't have and don't need.'

'I don't like the taste of it, but that's what Mose always does.'

Joe again silently sighed. He wished he didn't need to have this man-child along to guide him on his way, but perhaps by evening the hidden cache – whatever it contained – could be found and Dub sent on his way.

Silently, then, they broke camp, Joe saddling the weary old dun horse which eyed him with eyes that seemed offended by the thought of being ridden on this clear, cool day.

'That right there,' Dub said, swinging on to the red mare's back, 'is Mustang Ridge. Once we're over that we come down on to what they call Candlewick Creek. Want to know how Mustang Ridge got its name?'

'Not really,' Joe grunted as they started their horses forward up the rocky white-stone pass before them. The ridge, low but formidable-appearing, stood out starkly in the morning clearness. Dub was suddenly excited.

'A man told me how Candlewick got its name, too. He said it's because it's so narrow, can you believe that?'

'Yes,' Joe said. He thought himself a patient man, but Dub was trying that patience. As a traveling companion, the former chicken-wrangler left a lot to be desired. Joe had ridden long miles with men who had war stories to tell, tales of women loved and lost, once an old-timer named Ike Cavanaugh accompanied him as they rode the perimeter of the Double Seven, rounding up strays for the spring gather.

Cavanaugh, according to him, had once ridden with John Wesley Hardin, and had a lot of tales concerning the wild gunfighter's exploits. True or not, they livened up the days under the New Mexico sun in between rousting half-wild steers from their hidden canyon thickets.

No matter – Joe didn't have Cavanaugh or any of the old bunch riding with him. He had only Dub – and Dub knew the way to the cache of Pierce Malloy's 'ill-gotten' treasure.

Or Joe hoped he did.

It was difficult to tell with Dub. He seemed so utterly innocent of or unconcerned with the ways of the world, but he guided their way surely over broken, raw country until by mid afternoon they found themselves sitting on a ridge from which Joe could see the silver, snaking river which had to be Candlewick Creek.

'There's the place,' Dub said as they walked their horses across the creek, startling a young mule-deer buck on the far bank. Joe nodded. He could see the large grove of scattered oak trees indicated on Pierce Malloy's treasure map. Now it was a matter of finding the right spot.

There was supposed to be an 'X' carved on to one of the trees. 'Let's start searching for it,' Joe said, sliding down from his saddle. This could turn out to be a long, useless day after all. Or, he thought, perhaps it would lead to the conclusion of this long trek.

Dropping the reins to his dun to let it graze, he wandered among the oaks. The wind had increased, although it had grown warmer since leaving the ridge, and it ruffled the leaves of the oak trees with some vigor.

It took most of an hour, but they found it – or rather Dub found it and began whistling like some crazed prairie dog until Joe went to where he stood, pointing at the trunk of a large oak tree. The 'X' blazed into its bark was clearly visible, carved not long ago.

'Pirate treasure,' Dub panted, his mouth hanging open, eyes glittering dully.

'Yes,' was all Joe managed to say in answer. In truth he was probably as excited as Dub was – each for different reasons. Returning to the dun, Joe removed the spade from his pack and walked back to where the over-eager Dub waited as if standing guard. Joe glanced at the much-folded map he had been carrying in his pocket and saw, beside a drop of Malloy's blood, the scrawled words:

'Three long paces due north.'

Joe had no compass, of course, but he oriented himself northward as well as possible, using the high sun and the shadows sketched across the dark, leaf-littered earth. He walked nine feet from the base of the tree – three long strides and began looking for disturbed earth, Dub following him like an interested hound. Nothing was immediately evident, and so Joe began to move in an arc, using the point of his spade to search the ground.

He struck metal.

Muttering silently, he impatiently, energetically, began to probe, and the spade caught the edge of a small, flat metal box wrapped in oilskin and brought it to the surface. Dub fell on it, scrabbling at the earth with his bare fingers. He lifted the box skyward as if in veneration. Joe tossed his spade aside and took it from Dub's grubby hands.

'Open it,' Dub panted.

'I mean to – I hope it doesn't have a lock.'

'You can shoot it open,' Dub said, moving around Joe with manic energy. Apparently he had never seen lead bullets ricocheting off of a steel box or he wouldn't have said that. Strongboxes with their clasps of tempered steel are not so easily opened, or so Frank Cavanaugh said he had learned from his days with John Wesley Hardin.

Fortunately Joe did not have to prove or disprove this as the steel box, once unwrapped from the protective oilskin, had no lock, only a brass catch which, despite the care taken to protect it from the elements, held fast and refused to open.

'Gimme it. I'll open it,' Dub said, clutching at the air around Joe.

Joe said nothing. He pulled his belt knife from its sheath. The knife's blade was thick and unlikely to snap. Joe inserted the blade, wedged it a little tighter with the heel of his hand and twisted. The latch sprang free.

'I knew it!' Dub fairly screamed with delight. Joe was less demonstrative, but he, too, was slightly overwhelmed by what the box contained. From his knees where he had gone to pop the latch, he had opened the green box's lid to reveal sheaves of banded currency and two neat rows of gold coins stored in wooden racks.

'Tess Malloy,' Joe said, 'is going to be one happy woman.'

He closed the box then and refastened the latch despite the pleas of Dub who excitedly asked for one more look. There was no sense looking, no sense in counting what lay within the box. Having actually found the treasure, Joe wished for nothing more than to dispose of it. Newberry.

'Which way is Newberry now?' he asked Dub.

'Along the Candlewick, not far.'

Then Dub leaped up and began dancing in a crazy circle, whistling and shouting like a dervish. Joe didn't see what had gotten the kid so excited.

And then he did – from the creek bottom, Solomon and Moses were approaching, weapons at the ready.

There was no mistaking the two men from Pierce Point. Mose's wide frame and puffy face and Sol with his grim expression and sharp, unshaven jowls made it possible for Joe to identify them even at this distance. That and Dub's apparent joy at seeing the two familiar faces.

How had they found them? Had Dub somehow tipped them off about the possible hidden treasure? Joe thought back, but could not think of a moment when he had had the opportunity to do so. Perhaps Mose and Sol had decided on their own that Joe had more than he was willing to share after finding the silver money he had given to Addie. She might have sent them herself. Who knew! Maybe they had just decided to come hunting Joe down for the hell of it.

It didn't matter – they were here. And they would have to be dealt with. Joe doubted that matters could be cleared up with a handshake and a smile.

The two men wanted gold . . . and blood.

FIVE

There wasn't a lot that could be done. Joe stepped behind the broad, rough trunk of the big oak tree for cover. As he watched, Mose and Sol split up and began riding different routes, presumably to encircle him. Joe waited, Colt clutched tightly in his hand, thumb on the hammer, watching. He glanced behind him too late and could do nothing to avoid the staggering blow of the rock in Dub's hand. Joe hit the ground hard, but he did not feel it. He was already out cold.

He awoke when the sky was fading toward sundown, and sat up. He tried to stand, but the throbbing pain in his skull was enough to drive him back to a sitting position against the grass. There was a trickle of dry blood from his ear. His hair was in his eyes. He looked around, knowing what he would see:

Nothing.

The treasure box was gone, of course, and so was his old dun horse. His Colt lay near at hand and he scooped it up, though it was of no use at the moment. No target offered itself except for a scolding crow high in the oak tree. Joe couldn't have hit it even if he'd had a reason to try.

With the black bird still mocking, he turned, placed his hands against the base of the tree and clawed himself erect. His skull still pounded and a spiral of tiny colored dots spun behind his eyes as he panted his way to his feet.

He stood with his back against the tree, hands behind him pressed against the rough bark of the old oak. He feared that if he fell he might never rise again. The crow cawed one more insult and winged away. Joe rubbed his eyes and stared bleakly at the western sky. It was not yet splashed with sundown color, but it soon would be. Then it would go dark and cold, leaving Joe afoot in the night in unfamiliar country.

He pushed away from the oak and began staggering through the trees toward the creek that lay beyond. Why that direction instead of another, he could not have said – but he had to start on, and the best bet was that the robbers would head back toward Pierce Point the way they had come.

Why had Dub suddenly switched loyalties? He knew nothing else but the chicken ranch, Addie and the brutality of Sol and Moses. Perhaps he had been trying to please them.

More likely he had just been scared stiff of what they might do to him for running away, helping Joe in his escape.

It was a weird, blurry landscape Joe Sample trudged through. His head ached, his vision was confused. It was almost as if he were moving underwater. He could make out Mustang Ridge, across the creek. Rough and jagged against the skyline, it was far away, very far, and impossibly high.

Joe waded the creek, his legs rubbery, his vision still blurred. Around him peeper frogs had begun their night chorusing. The current was swift against his boots, making the going even more uncertain. The rocks underfoot were slick, but he managed to make it to the far bank. There he had no choice but to sit and rest, his head hanging between his knees in exhaustion.

How could he expect to go – across the Mustang Ridge, all the way back to Pierce Point with night already settling. It didn't seem unlikely; it seemed impossible. Why had he ever put himself in this position? The sky darkened; the night birds began to call; the river continued to trickle past. And. . . .

A horse nickered nearby!

Joe scooted up the bank, took hold of a willow branch and somehow managed to leverage himself to his feet. He stood in the silence, listening and watching. Something moved through the willow brush and Joe dropped his hand to reach for his gun, eyes straining. Then he saw the animal – the dun, its saddle canted over to one side, emerged from the underbrush and fixed accusing eyes on Joe.

They had cut the dun loose, there being no point in continuing to lead it along their way. It would only slow them up and complicate matters. Joe approached the dun slowly, speaking soothingly. When he reached it, he took a firm grip on its bridle and stroked its neck. The saddle cinches were not broken, but only loose. In the scabbard on the saddle was Joe's Winchester rifle. His saddle-bags had been rifled, but there had been nothing of value there to be taken. Probably in disgust, they had left the dun behind.

'Stand,' Joe said hopefully to the horse, and feeling weaker than he could ever remember, he positioned the saddle and tugged the cinches tight. He had a riding animal again.

What help that could possibly be, he could not have said. He would have to track down armed men over broken country he was unfamiliar with and somehow retrieve the stolen money, then backtrack toward Newberry and attempt to find Tess Malloy.

He wasn't up to it, not in his present shape. It took nearly all of his physical reserves just to climb into the saddle and start the old dun horse back along the uncertain trail toward Pierce Point.

Joe was following the sun and as he rose from the darkness that had settled into the canyon bottom, he met a much more brilliantly-lighted sky. Cresting the ridge on the weary dun horse he found the sun almost blinding before him as it settled toward the horizon. Around him the snaking canyons were in pools of darkness; to the south the white desert sands glittered with heated light.

Neither terrain was appealing to his eye. The horse shuddered beneath him and Joe stroked its neck. Neither of them was up to many more miles of rough riding. A cold anger rode with Joe, however, and he was driven to push on. One more ridge and then another – he had long since lost a memory of the trail he and Dub had followed on the way over the hills and now rode by instinct alone, urging the dun forward. One ridge followed another, a row of white stone, naked rises, alike in their barrenness, uniform dryness and steep thrust. Joe felt like a fool, a weary, exhausted fool with a massive headache. But he felt compelled to continue as long as there was sun in the sky.

When he crested what must have been the third or fourth such ridge he suddenly halted the exhausted dun and stood in the stirrups. Before him lay a dry valley in shadow, and camped there was a group of men, their horses trying to forage for graze on the infertile land.

Three men, he saw, as they moved around the dry camp. He had found his quarry. He recognized Dub, wandering with the horses as if he, too, were foraging. Sol and Mose were crouched close together, their faces turned down intently. It seemed they were counting the stolen money. Or that could have been Joe's imagination, as the men were too far distant to tell for sure, but it made sense.

He could picture the excitement, their self-congratulation. No more chicken ranch; money to gamble with, to make friends with young women, to buy fine horses and clothes with. Never to have to work again drudging for Adelaide Comfort. The image caused Joe's blood to begin simmering again despite his trail-weariness and the ache in his skull where a knot the size of a hen's egg had developed.

Mentally the two had already spent most of Tess Malloy's fortune. Joe intended to destroy their pipe dreams.

They were in deep shadow and Joe on a brightly-lit ridge where he would make an easy target silhouetted against the skyline, and so he guided the dun into a shallow feeder canyon, just deep enough to hide horse and man. He drew his rifle from its scabbard, figuring he would need all the extra firepower available. He still wasn't sure how he was going to take the two armed men down – that would just have to play itself out. He discounted Dub, not because he trusted him, but because he went unarmed – unless he was near enough to use a rock.

Nearing the canyon floor Joe thought he could hear voices, indistinguishable, of course, but not far off. He hoped that they were not listening close enough to make out the clopping of the dun's hoofs.

Emerging from harsh light into near-darkness Joe pulled up his horse for a few minutes to let his eyes adjust. He cuffed the perspiration from his eyes, took several deep breaths and slid from the saddle. On impulse he decided to try a distraction in his planned attack.

He loosened the twin cinches on his saddle and then canted the saddle over into the position it had been in when he found the dun. The horse eyed him balefully. It had thought itself ready to be unsaddled and now had to endure this new indignity.

Joe swatted the horse on the rump and then made his own way toward the camp, ducking behind the boulders which had fallen from the bluffs over the years.

Solomon who had been busy shoving the green

strongbox into his saddle-bags lying on the ground nearby heard something and rose to his feet, his hand lowering toward his holstered pistol.

'What's that?' he hissed and Moses turned toward him.

'What are you talking about?'

'I heard something coming this way – a horse.'

Both men stood staring into the darkness. Moses had his shotgun up and ready. Now both could clearly hear an approaching horse. 'Who do you think it could be?' Sol asked in a whisper.

'It could be anybody – stand away a little.'

They spread apart and stood ready to defend their new-found wealth against any intruder. From out of the darkness the abused dun horse staggered toward their camp, its saddle askew. Sol laughed out loud.

'Damned if the old nag didn't follow us,' he said, holstering his pistol. Dub had come to join them.

'Poor horse,' he said, 'let me get that saddle off him.'

'Go ahead,' Moses told him. 'Stupid old horse has more heart than sense.'

'He couldn't have lasted long out there with that saddle all tilted,' Dub put in, but neither of the others answered. They seldom bothered to answer Dub.

'Can I have him?' Dub asked hopefully.

'You've got the red mare,' Moses said.

'But this one's got a saddle. I like him.'

'If he can make it back to Pierce Point, I guess you can keep him,' Moses said, feeling generous now that he and Sol were rich men. At least the kid hadn't asked for a cut of the money. He knew he couldn't have any of it. Let him keep the old dun pony.

They both tensed again as a voice, unexpected yet somehow familiar called from out of the shadows:

'Stand steady, boys, and shed your guns!'

Solomon glanced at Moses as if to ask, 'Can you see him?' but Moses shook his head. The night was filled with shadows, and the voice belonged to one among many of the vague silhouettes.

'Did you hear me?' Joe called again as the two men hesitated. 'I want you to drop those guns or die.'

Then Joe who had been creeping closer stepped on a small round rock and slipped. The movement was enough to distinguish his shadow from the others, and Sol cried out.

'I see him!' and he drew his sidearm.

Joe was down on one knee with his rifle aimed at Solomon, but still Sol went blazing away with his .44 revolver – he was that kind of a man. Sol's bullets flew wildly across the valley, although one of them came close enough to tug at Joe's shirt sleeve. That was enough for Joe, who triggered off the Winchester, his shot true and effective. Solomon staggered back a little, lifted his eyes to the dark sky and crumpled up.

Moses, having located Joe by the flare of his muzzle, opened up with his shotgun. The scatter-gun emitted smoke and flame and the pellets from it flew past Joe who had flung himself to the ground as Moses shouldered his weapon. Moses drew back the hammer of his second barrel, and Joe shot him. Moses grunted an indecipherable curse and loosed off his second shot, sending buckshot into the sky, briefly lighting the night with devil fire as he backed up, sat down and tilted over on his side.

Joe waited, levering a fresh round into the Winchester's breech, but neither of the two men moved. Slowly he got to his feet and lurched forward. Dub came staggering toward him from out of the night.

'Don't shoot me! I ain't got no gun,' Dub shouted with panic.

'I'm not going to shoot you,' Joe Sample growled.

'Joe? Is that you, Joe? I'm sorry I hit you with that rock. I don't know why I did it!'

'Just get out of here,' Joe barked, 'Get back to the chicken ranch.'

'What about Mose and Sol? You still got that

spade? I could bury them.'

'Leave them, or put them on the horses if the animals will tolerate it. Just get out of here, Dub! I hope to never see you again.'

'Joe, I—'

'Get out of here!' Joe's voice thundered. Then in a more reasonable tone he told the young man. 'Addie will be needing your help more than ever now. You still haven't sprayed those flies in the chicken coop.'

'Are you going to steal the horses, Joe?' Dub asked.

'I'm going to need one of them – the black, I suppose.'

'Sol's horse?' the kid asked doubtfully. 'He wouldn't like that.'

'I'm going to trade for him – the dun for the black. Now get busy, will you? I've got a headache, and I'm just tired of talking to you.'

As Joe sat cross-legged on the ground and watched, Dub went about his work as if it were an everyday task and nothing unusual had happened. He first positioned the dun's saddle again then carried the bodies of Solomon and Moses to the red mare and the gray, which was Moses' horse. Joe waited unhappily, watching. He took the few usable items from the saddle-bags on the dun, shifted them to the pouches carried by the black horse with three white stockings and added the

72

strongbox. Although any stunt by Dub was extremely unlikely at this point, Joe kept his eye on him, making sure for example that he did not get hold of the weapons belonging to Moses and Solomon.

'Well,' Dub said eventually, from the back of the dun horse. 'I'll be getting, though Addie won't like the sight of me bringing these two home dead.' He brightened: 'I guess she'll be bound to scramble me up a mess of eggs, though!'

'So long, Dub,' Joe muttered and he slapped the dun on the haunch, sending the aged animal on its way. Dub leading the other two horses.

Now what?

Joe was trail-weary and half sick. There were a few items in his saddle-bags, but he did not feel like starting a fire out here and cooking. Who knew what idea might present itself to Dub's mind. He approached the black horse again. The animal was used to only one rider, it seemed, and was not so sure about Joe. But it was younger, slightly fresher than the dun had been. It would have to get used to the idea that Joe meant to ride it.

He had to again reach the Candlewick, if he could find it, then follow its course northward until he could find Newberry or at least some local citizens who knew where the town lay. There was still a young widow out there in need of the comfort the money might provide. That, after all, was what he had set out to do, and it had to be done.

Joe Sample's leg had begun to ache again to top everything off. It was healed well enough, but this long riding was doing it no good. Joe swung aboard the balky black horse and started it forward. There was only moonlight to ride by now, and he was following an uncertain course. He made his weary way across the rugged hills, his mind fixed on the rest and the meals he could catch up on back at the Double Seven, at the end of the trail.

SIX

The morning light was pleasant and bright on the slow-flowing water of Candlewick Creek. The sun was warm and welcome on his back and shoulders. The night before when he knew he could not go on, he had camped out in a cold hollow along one of the mountain ridges, the black horse's lead tied to his foot. It had been a miserable night. He had awakened hungry and shivering long before the sun had begun to rise. Now he was beginning to have some hope of success in his enterprise. The younger horse was fresh and seemingly eager. Joe's angry stomach's complaints were fewer. He guided the black downslope toward the creek where he loosened the saddle and let it drink.

There was even a patch of grass growing near the creek, of a sort Joe did not recognize, but which the horse nibbled at contentedly while Joe lazed in the morning shade beneath a stand of willows. The day was warming quickly, but his proximity to water allowed him to remain comfortably cool. The breeze had again begun to stir with the advent of morning but in the shelter of the creek bottom it was not the harsh wind of the day before. It did nothing but turn up the silver undersides of the willow leaves in its passing. Plus it kept the insects down.

After the horse had rested for an hour, Joe again tightened his cinches and started north, following the silver-flowing Candlewick. At times the walls of the bluffs rising from the creek narrowed so much that he had to walk his horse through the shallow river water, but the black did not seem to mind – perhaps it cooled its feet.

It was in the middle of the afternoon that Joe came upon a scattering of homes. Not so large as Pierce Point – there was no apparent business district – it seemed nevertheless to be an established settlement. Was this Newberry? He guided the black horse, which he had come to like for its vigor and agility, up out of the creek plain and on to the dry grassland which surrounded the scattered houses, occasional outbuildings and corrals he saw there.

The first person he came across was an old man with a white beard leading a reluctant goat with a beard much like that of its captor. The man wore a blue-checked cotton shirt, out at the elbows, jeans and a straw hat which looked as if the goat had been at it. There was also a red kerchief around his neck and as Joe Sample approached, the man untied it and stood wiping his forehead and throat with it.

'What do you want?' the old man asked as Joe drew the black horse to a halt. The goat used this opportunity to try to draw away, but the old man held the line tight in his gnarled hand.

'Nothing,' Joe said with a smile and a shrug, 'I'm just trying to find my way to Newberry.'

'Why?' the old-timer asked as the goat bleated.

'My own business,' Joe answered.

'There ain't nothin' there,' the man advised him.

'No?'

'No,' the old man said severely. 'I ought to know, because this is Newberry.'

'In that case, you might be able to tell me where I can find the Malloy place.'

The old man's mouth puckered, his eyes drifted away. He gave his perspiring throat one more wipe and then lifted his bony shoulders and asked, 'Why do you want to find it?'

'My own business,' Joe said again.

'I can tell you, young feller. What you do is go straight ahead, find the Old Post Road. Anybody will tell you where it is if you can't locate it. Then you ride about two miles east. You'll find the Malloy place on your right. They got a pair of white-washed stone markers by the road leading to their house. You got me so far?'

'Yes, I think so.' Joe replied.

'You go past them markers and keep on going as far as your pony will carry you,' the old man advised him. 'There's nothing out there but thieves and killers. Those Malloys! If you're not one of 'em, if you're an honest man, you don't want anything to do with 'em. That's my advice to you; if you have any sense, you'll take it.'

'Are you talking about Pierce and Amos? Because if you haven't heard—'

'I'm talkin' about the whole damn bunch of them! Nothin' but a nest of thieves and killers. Take my advice, young man. Come along, Billy! You've been wandering long enough. Time to get you home.'

The conversation was at an end. The old man trudged off toward a small, red-roofed farmhouse, tugging the reluctant billy goat behind him.

After two false starts, Joe Sample found the Old Post Road an hour later.

The day was cooling, the wind had ceased. It was still light but there was a splash of pale pink on the high thin clouds to the west when Joe Sample found the two rock pillars daubed with whitewash flanking a rough narrow road that led, he supposed, on to Malloy property.

He sat the black horse, resting it and thinking. He wondered how seriously he ought to take the warnings of the man with the goat. After all, he knew none of these people – and he was carrying money, a lot of it.

But his intention was to give it to Tess Malloy anyway; why should anyone want to do him harm when he had arrived to do them a favor? Her, least of all. Whatever sort of agreement she had with the others, what their relationship was, was none of Joe's affair. Perhaps they were relatives of hers. Perhaps she owed some of them money. That was something for Tess Malloy to handle. For himself, he felt that he was safe – he had never heard of a robber walking up to a man who was approaching with open hands and threatening him.

If they did, Joe felt now that he no longer cared. He had been forced to kill a couple of men; he had ridden a long trail with a sore leg and an aching head. He only wanted to be done with it all, his obligation satisfied, and make his slow journey homeward, to Socarro and the Double Seven Ranch.

The Malloy house could not be seen from the road but after cresting a low knoll, Joe was able to make it out, standing alone among a stand of pepper trees and acacia bushes. The two kinds of shrubs made a pretty little border for the property – the trees with their red berries, the yellow blooming flowers of the mimosa acacia shrubs adding color to an otherwise barren section of land.

To one side of the white adobe house was a stand of nopal cactus, their apples still green, but perhaps planted there for the color they would bring when the cactus apples turned red. Across the front of the house a long tendril of thorny bougainvillea crossed the length of the house's face like a brightly colored purple-red brow. Someone had taken the trouble to try to add color to this desert land where there was little otherwise.

Swinging down in front of the house, he noticed the low white-painted stone border in front of it guarded white and blue lupine. This had to be a woman's doing, all of it. Men just didn't appreciate color as they did. Maybe that had something to do with the idea that a courting man should take his woman a bouquet of flowers – Joe didn't know.

The house porch, broad but narrow, was supported by four native stone pillars, all freshly daubed with whitewash. Leaving the strongbox where it rode in his saddle-bags for the time being, Joe stepped up on to the porch, removed his hat and knocked on the door. Looking around he saw no other people, no other horses. The sky was still faintly coloring. A bee buzzed past Joe's eyes.

The door opened and Joe found himself looking into the deep blue eyes of a perfectly made young, dark-haired woman. She resembled a porcelain doll with her wide eyes and tiny well-rounded body. He had to swallow before he spoke.

'Mrs Malloy?'

'I'm Tess Malloy.'

'My name is Joe Sample. I've come bringing you some bad news, and some good.'

'They hung Amos,' the young woman behind the screen door said, almost expressionlessly.

'Well . . . yes,' Joe answered, not sure what else to say.

'I knew it,' Tess said. 'I don't know how Pierce thought he could stop it.'

'Pierce . . .' Joe began.

'They got him, too?'

'Yes. I'm afraid so. Gunned him down – I was there when it happened.'

'They never learn, this family,' Tess said with a sigh. She unhooked the latch on the screen door and opened it to admit the stranger with his hat in hand.

'Come in and have a cool glass of water. I appreciate your coming all this way to tell me, although I had already come to terms with the idea that it was inevitable.'

'I would appreciate the water. Then I'll need some for my horse. First, though, I'd like to give you something that Pierce sent. I'd like to get it off my hands and off my conscience.'

'What is it, money?' Tess asked with a sort of patient weariness. Joe squinted at the girl, a little puzzled by her reaction. 'They always thought that was the solution to everything,' Tess explained. 'I couldn't think of anything else Pierce would think to send me.'

'Well, yes,' Joe said in a faltering voice, 'that's what it is – money. Quite a bit of it.'

'All right. Bring it in then, although there won't be enough to buy my husband's life back, will there?'

'No, not that much,' Joe said. He found himself wondering what sort of life Tess had been living if this was indeed an outlaws' hideout and her husband, Amos, had been among them. Always watching out for the law, wondering who would make it home alive? It was no wonder that she scorned the gift of money. For some reason he thought of Desiree Delfino who had thought that money would buy her respectability in Yuma.

None of what might have happened to Tess Malloy was his business either. He walked to the black horse, extracted the strongbox from the saddle-bags and returned.

The interior of the house was dark, a little

musty, and not particularly cool. Joe began following Tess across the hardwood floor toward the interior. He made it three steps before he heard a muffled sound behind him and had a blurred glimpse of a man stepping from behind the door to club him down.

It was dark when Joe awoke, barely able to achieve a sitting position. It was as if the house had a tilted floor which slowly rotated beneath him. He simply sat there in the murk of night. His head, which seemed to be everyone's favorite target, ached and throbbed. Fortunately – or maybe not – the man who had clubbed him had struck the opposite side of his skull from where Dub had used his rock. Everyone had always told him that he had a thick skull, perhaps now that was proving fortunate.

Joe rolled over with a groan and made his way on hands and knees to a cowhide-covered sofa which he used to assist him to his feet. The house was silent. He had the vaguest of memories of horses having been ridden away from the rear of the house, but that might have been delusion.

Where was Tess!

That started his blood pulsing quicker. Had someone stolen the money, and worse, stolen away with her? He started slowly, clumsily, toward the interior of the house. Moonlight shone through a window there, blue and faint. It was the kitchen, he saw as he stood there, using his hands against the doorframe to brace himself. There was no sign of Tess, no indication of a struggle. The room, arranged around a round, sawn-plank table was as neat as a pin. Joe stumbled across to the kitchen door and looked out into the night. The moon cast shadows beneath a shaggy pepper tree. A kit fox – or some other small animal – scuttled away.

Joe wiped his hand across his face. He was weary, plain tired. Perhaps the latest blow to his head was making him feel that way, but he was dizzy and ready to pass out. Yet he knew that remaining in this house was not wise. Maybe he should have listened to the goat man.

At any moment the man who had clubbed him down could return to finish the job. There might have been a swarm of bandits using the place for a hideout. Joe had no way of knowing. He was determined to leave, but first, he had to find out if Tess was still here, in some sort of trouble.

He started moving through the house in the dark, pistol in hand.

The floors of the house creaked under his boots. The same murky blue light glimmered from the rising moon in all of the rooms. Joe eased down the hallway, keeping his hands on the side of the wall nearest him. Each door he came to opened on nothing but darkness. Each had a high, narrow window and a neatly made bed. There was no human warmth lingering in the place.

There was a faint tapping from somewhere and a furtive scurrying, like rats moving about.

But nothing human. He began to believe that whoever had struck him must have taken Tess with him. Poor little wide-eyed girl.

He continued on his way, coming at last to a broad room, twice the size of the others – the master bedroom, where all was in neat order, patchwork quilt smoothed over a double bed. No one there. Joe took a deep breath, touched fingers to his bloody head and started back up the hall, wishing to be out of there before someone returned.

The tapping came again.

Joe frowned and inched forward. Halfway along the hallway he brushed what seemed to be a knob and glanced down, He could barely make out the door to a half cupboard set low in the wall.

The tapping came again, more urgently and he could now tell that it was coming from inside the tiny cupboard. There was a barrel-latch on the door and he slid it open, holding his revolver at the ready. Opening the door he saw by the faint light of the moon through the windows, the huddled figure of a woman with tangled red hair, her hands bound behind her, ankles tied, gag over her mouth.

Joe crouched down and removed the gag as

wide, frightened eyes watched him. The woman gasped for air, coughed once and licked at her dry lips.

'Who are you?' Joe asked, trying to untie the tight knots in the rope that bound her ankles.

'I'm Tess Malloy,' the red-haired girl answered.

'But if you are Tess Malloy, who was. . . ?' Joe asked as the two sat at the kitchen table, the girl rubbing her chafed wrists.

'That was Marcie. Marcie Epps. Pretty little thing, isn't she? So pretty that men believe anything she says. That's one weakness all of you seem to share.'

'Who hit me?' Joe Sample wanted to know.

'That was Trace Balmer. He was the only one at home. He and lovely Marcie had a little something going on between them. They talked about leaving together now and then.' The girl – Tess – had wide green eyes which she kept fixed on Joe's as she spoke. She, too, was a nice-looking woman with a dusting of freckles across her nose and cheeks. Her hands, Joe noticed, were slightly work-roughened as Marcie's had not been.

'They took the money.'

'Of course – running away to some lovers' paradise; no need to split it with the rest of the gang.'

'How could they have known that I was coming, that I had the money?' Joe asked, puzzled.

'The news of what happened came over the wire yesterday – we're a modern town now, we even have a telegraph line. The boys – by that I mean Cornish, Stiles, and Frank Singleton, were off looking for a bank to rob. Trace Banner, as I told you, stayed behind to be with Marcie. When they found out that my husband had been hanged and that Pierce had died in a shoot-out with the local law, they talked things over. Trace, well all of them, really, had told Pierce not to try dealing with the warden down in Yuma. He was new on the job, not the old one who had gotten fat enough on bribes to retire.

'What they actually wanted, of course, was the money – I never did learn where that came from. Amos never told me, and none of the others had said either. They always clammed up when I was around, I suppose so that I could never provide any evidence against them. I have an idea or two where the strongbox came from, but I could be wrong. . . .

'Anyway,' Tess said, now rubbing the ankle of the leg she had crossed over the other. 'Pierce told them all pretty much to go to hell. "I'll not see my brother given to the hangman if I can stop it!" is what he told them, and no one was going to argue with Pierce when he was in a bad mood. He was the leader, of course, and the men did what he said.'

'Then what?' Joe asked. 'Marcie and Trace waited to see what would happen?'

'They knew Pierce. We all did. They had discussed that if Pierce couldn't get to the warden he would find a way of getting the money back to us. He had told us that before he left. Well, some of the gang didn't believe that. They took the money for a lost cause, but I knew he would find a way to do it if he could – Pierce was a hard man and a deadly one, but he always kept his word. Otherwise he wouldn't have gone to Yuma in the first place. He had a . . . sense of honor. Unusual in such a rough man, but he did.'

Tess placed her foot down and smoothed her off-pink skirt. Salmon-colored, or something, women would call it, he thought irrelevantly. Joe was aware again of his limited knowledge of or concern about colors.

'Then they just sat and waited for me, or someone like me to come?'

'Pretty much. Of course we can see anyone approaching for a long way – one reason why Pierce and Amos chose this place for a hideout. It doesn't take a lot of attentiveness to keep watch. Then, when they saw you, the likely dupe – sorry to use that word – coming, they tied and gagged me and stuffed me in the little closet.'

'Why?'

'Why? Because I knew what they had planned.

Taking the money and running before Frank Singleton and the other boys could get back.'

'When will that be?' Joe asked with some apprehension. He glanced toward the front door although he would certainly have heard the arrival of horses.

'That all depends on what kind of luck they have been having. Tonight, if everything went smoothly and no one got shot or cornered by the law . . . you never know when they'll show up.'

'Tess? Is this the sort of life you like?'

'It's the sort I fell into. I didn't know much about Amos when I married him. He told me he was a horse trader by profession. He was tall, with curly hair and an easy laugh. I was a very young girl. Now,' she spread her hands, 'I just can't leave. There's no place for me but here.'

'Without money?' Joe said, pursuing the point.

'Without money.' she said and he saw a tear glistening in her eye. She buried her face in her hands and shook her head. Her thin shoulders trembled a little.

Joe stood, walked behind her and put a hand on her shoulder. When she looked up, he asked:

'Where were they going? Marcie and Trace Banner, I mean.'

'They always talked of Flagstaff. Marcie has family up there. Why? Why do you ask, Joe?'

'I thought maybe I would just travel along that

89

way, and see what I can do about getting that money back,' he said. 'It's not only men like Pierce Malloy who have a sense of honor.'

SEVEN

The land rose higher and cooled as Joe made his way toward Flagstaff. Cedar trees and pines, sometimes standing in thick stands along the flanks of the mountains, became more common. To the north the pines grew by the thousands, forming a sea of green moving with the breeze. There were a hundred little rivulets and sheer waterfalls rushing off the granite of the hillside. Joe let the horse walk lazily up the long slope; there was no point in racing madly after Marcie and Trace Banner. They likely would not be hurrying either, certain that their plan had worked and they had outdistanced any possible pursuit.

Distantly Joe could now see the town of Flagstaff set prettily among the tall timber. He had to find the family home of the Eppses – that was where Tess believed they had gone. She was probably right. In the other direction lay the long desert and Yuma, neither of which they would be likely to attempt, especially since, according to Tess, the remnants of the Malloy gang: Frank Singleton, Cornish and Stiles, had apparently ridden out in that direction intending more mischief. There were not many roads across the desert, and the chances of running into the returning gang were too great to be ignored.

Joe kept his black horse to its easy pace, although now as they neared the town, the animal began trying to pull ahead, perhaps sensing other horses or anticipating the opportunity to enjoy decent fodder after its haphazard foraging of the past few days.

They made their way down a long slope, Joe sizing up the town. It was larger than he remembered. A lot of other people were finding it attractive, it seemed. Along the main street and four or five side streets, false-fronted buildings, and a few of yellow brick, had sprouted up. These were the stores, stables, banks, hotels and general stores. Flagstaff had no intention of withering and blowing away like the tiny desert towns on the long flats beyond.

Where first?

Joe hated to start asking around randomly about the Epps family. Perhaps they, too, were an outlaw bunch – he didn't want to give anyone a hint of his intentions. The black horse had made its own intentions clear as they approached a stable along the bustling main street. It wanted fresh hay and oats and some time from under the saddle. Joe realized that he could also use some food and rest, some time out of the saddle, if he were to do his work efficiently. His head had almost stopped aching, but his leg was getting worse, healed improperly as it was.

He mentally counted the little silver money he had remaining in his jeans – the scant amount Tittle Sparks had not been able to steal as he slept. It should be enough both to board the horse and to feed himself.

It was evening already when Joe walked from the stable. Through the pines he could see a long crimson banner of sheer cloud against the sundown skies. He trudged uptown, looking for an inexpensive restaurant. There must be many there, as crowded as the town seemed to be with workmen and cowboys who would need to be fed.

It was nearly full dark before he found the sort of place he was looking for. Long plank tables resting on wooden barrels ran along both sides of the interior and a trio of high-aproned, weary-appearing waitresses moved between them, carrying platters of beef, potatoes and biscuits. Nothing fancy, of course, but enough to fill the stomachs of working men who had been hard at it all day long. Joe found a spot near the end of one of the benches and sat down.

Everyone was drinking coffee, though a few of the men were doctoring it up with whiskey, so Joe ordered a cup plus whatever the usual fare was. Then he sat silently watching the throng, his elbows on the table, clasped hands under his chin.

Joe was served a smallish steak and a mound of fried potatoes. The meat was tougher than he would have liked, but he was hungry enough not to care much. Beside him a whiskered, lantern-jawed man finished his meal, stretched and leaned back in his chair, smiling vaguely at Joe.

'The apple pie's good here,' the stranger said.

'Is it?'

'I'm going to order a slab to finish off my supper.'

Joe nodded as he sawed at his meat. Then, deciding he would have to begin his search somewhere, he asked:

'Are you from around here?'

'Most of my life,' the stranger acknowledged, holding up a finger toward a waitress who apparently knew what he wanted by the gesture, scribbled on her pad and went away to the kitchen.

Chewing, Joe said, 'Do you know some people named Epps living in the area?'

'Epps? Yeah, I know them.'

'Do you know where they live?'

'Not far. Have you business with them?'

'Yes, I do,' Joe answered, pushing his plate away as the harried waitress returned with his neighbor's slice of apple pie. 'Can you tell me where their home is?'

'It's out a way,' the man said, cutting into his pie with his fork. 'Not so easy to describe.' Around a mouthful of apple pie, he said, 'I wouldn't mind taking you out there – I've got nothing else to do.'

'I'd appreciate that,' Joe said.

'I'll tell you what: pick up the check for my supper and I'll show you out there. Just let me get my horse.'

'All right,' Joe agreed with relief. He wondered if he had enough money left to pay for two meals, figured he did and said, 'My own horse is at the A-1 stable. I'll meet you over there in half an hour.'

'You got a deal,' the stranger said, wiping his mouth with his napkin. 'I'll be there.'

The two shook hands and the stranger recovered his hat from a row of pegs along the wall behind them before strolling out. Joe finished his own meal quickly and dipped into his pocket, silently counting his change. He took what was needed to the cashier behind the small counter and told the woman that he would be paying for two. He waited while the bills were totted up, paid, grabbed a toothpick from the glass jar filled with them and walked out into the cool of night, headed for the stable.

The black horse looked up at him unhappily as he entered the A-1, but seemed resigned to traveling on as it was saddled.

'I brushed him down pretty good,' the chubby stableman said with a touch of pride. 'Looks all glossy now, don't he?'

'He looks fine,' Joe said. If the man was hinting for a tip, he was out of luck.

Joe's leg had begun hurting again. He wasn't eager to swing back into the saddle, so he led the black out the door and stood waiting in the darkness for his dinner companion to arrive. The moon was settling wearily in the west, dropping behind the long ranks of pines on the peaks beyond the town. People passed. Across the street two sedate looking business types walked the plankwalk, arm in arm with two well-dressed ladies. Along the boulevard a trio of roistering cowboys raced from one end of main street to the other.

The stranger from the restaurant did not appear.

Nor did he come in the next hour. Joe figured he had been hoodwinked. He did not blame a man down on his luck for cadging a meal, but he had cost Joe valuable time. It was getting to be too late to accomplish anything. He led the black into the stable again, unsaddled under the puzzled squint of the man there, and went off to look for a place to catch some sleep.

At first light Joe left the boarding house where he had spent the night with eight or ten other hard-luck men and began walking the streets. The courthouse was a red-brick, two-storied affair with four young elm trees planted at equal distances before it. Obviously new, the building was probably the town pride. He mounted the steps and went in. The courthouse was not open yet, but Joe searched the neatly-painted directory, and found what he wanted. The records division would certainly have a list of all local landowners, and maps of the area. Joe found a seat on the polished wooden bench in front of the office and sat down to wait.

Two men, both wearing badges passed him by, boot heels clicking against the oak flooring. The taller of the two, a man with neatly parted hair, wearing a red shirt and brown twill trousers, wore the distinctive badge of a United States marshal. Joe had only seen one such ever before, down in Phoenix. Neither man even glanced his way as he sagged further on to the bench, feeling distinctly guilty. As he thought about it, perhaps he did have reasons to be uneasy around the men with the tin stars: the stolen money he had been transporting, the deaths of Solomon and Moses at his hands. . . . The two men entered a room at the end of the hall, closed the door and were gone from sight.

Joe rubbed his face with his hands, tilted his head back and waited for the county clerks to arrive.

Half an hour later, Joe was on his way again. The friendly if drowsy clerks in the land office had shown him the small, twenty-acre parcel which was the Epps family holding. It was only a few miles out of town, he had been told, on a seasonal creek called the Tropic, on the sunrise side of Flagstaff.

The black, perhaps feeling better after its feeding, moved out eagerly across the hum-mocked land where the pines were thinner, but the grass thicker. Joe passed several small man-made ponds where disinterested cattle and a few horses glanced up at him. The black horse thought they should investigate some of the standing stock which included some young mares, but Joe kept the animal's head pointed straight ahead, kneeing it onward.

Shortly before noon he came upon the small white house. It looked as described on the prop-erty lists – square, low-built. It had a green roof and was surrounded by an insignificant barn and half a dozen outbuildings: a smokehouse, tool shed and henhouse among them. Beyond the house was a corral and to one side, in the shade of the trees, a pigsty.

There were four horses in the corral, but none tied at the hitchrail before the house, and no people evident as Joe made his way cautiously through the stand of pines toward the house. No smoke rose from the stone chimney. A red dog yapped at him once and then scurried away, hiding its tail between its legs.

Deciding not to call out to the house in case someone was watching for him over a rifle's gun-sights, Joe eased the black horse to the sundown side of the place and dropped its reins, swinging down in the yard to ease his way around to the front door.

No one called out, and he could hear no one moving about inside or out. Either no one was there or they were waiting to confront him. The owners of the house, he knew from the records he had seen, were Rachel and John Epps. What relationship, if any, they had with the Malloy gang, he could not guess.

In the front of the house where a tall twin pine tree stood, Joe eased up on to the wooden porch. He crouched low under the front window and moved to the door, his hand on his gun. He would have drawn it but he had not come with the intention of frightening older, innocent people. He only wanted to find Marcie, Trace Banner and Tess's stolen money. He rapped on the door and waited impatiently.

It seemed a long time before he heard beyond the white-painted door, the shuffling of feet, slow unsteady movements and a muffled sound like a hiccup. The door swung suddenly open and Joe found himself facing an old woman who walked with a cane. Her hair was white, tied back in a bun, her small eyes blue and foxy. She could be Marcie's mother, probably was. Although the woman was old she did not seem to have collected any of the flab on her body that age can deliver. Small, seemingly brightly alert, she smiled at Joe and asked briskly:

'What would you be wanting, young fellow?'

'I came looking for Marcie . . . and Trace Banner. If they're here, I'd like to talk to them.'

'I see.' The old woman's blue eyes narrowed. 'Are you a member of the Malloy Company, then?'

It took Joe a moment to compose his answer. 'No, but I've had dealings with them.' The old woman seemed to have been convinced that the Malloy gang was some legitimate business concern in which her daughter held an interest. She smiled at Joe.

'Well, come in out of the sun. I'm the only one home just now. They've gone off somewhere – you know how young people are. My name's Rachel Epps, by the way. I'm Marcie's mother.' On her cane she hobbled toward the back of the house, where apparently the kitchen lay.

'Sit down, young man.' she called. 'I've got a fresh pitcher of spring water to cool you down.

Then we can talk, if you like, or you can just sit and wait for Marcie to get back. I understand there has been some sort of problem with the ownership,' she called around the corner as Joe found a seat on a worn green sofa. 'One of the managers passed away?'

Joe again had to pause to frame an answer. Finally he said, 'I think that's what happened. I myself am working for Tess Malloy – it's a personal matter.'

'I see.' Rachel Epps emerged from the kitchen, holding a silver tray in one hand. It held a glass of water and a small stack of oatmeal cookies. 'I thought you might like a bite to eat,' she said. 'A young man like you. I'm sorry I can't offer you a proper meal, but breakfast's already done and I've just now finished cleaning up after,' She placed the tray down gingerly on the small table beside the sofa.

'There's no need to apologize,' Joe said. He took one of the cookies and bit into it. It was very good, rich with molasses. He turned to say so to Rachel when he saw the old woman, her mouth twisted into a tight grimace wielding a black fireplace poker. She had it raised high with both hands, ready to club down with it. Joe's first thought was:

Not my head again!

He spun away, overturning the tray on the

table and threw up a protective arm as the poker arced down at his head. He would never have thought that such a small, elderly woman could deliver a blow with so much force, but the poke, driving down from overhead struck his shoulder with enough force to temporarily deaden his arm.

'For God's sake!' Rachel screamed out. 'Why don't all you people just leave us alone!'

With her rage expired, her strength seemed to leave her. She staggered forward one step and then fell to the floor, the poker clattering free. Joe Sample managed to pick the woman up and stretch her out on the sofa. When she came around, she clutched at her breast, her throat and then put her hand to her mouth. Joe gave her a sip of the water she had brought to him. Then he sat down facing her.

'Why did you try to hit me?'

'Why?' she asked drily. 'They told me that men were after them – killers.'

'You mean Marcie and Trace Banner told you that?'

'That's right. My daughter. She said that she and Trace were trying to make a break from the gang.'

'Where'd they go?' Joe asked.

'Into town to buy a carriage. They're going down to Tucson – that's where Trace is from. They're going to buy a house there and live like

102

honest folks.'

Joe said nothing to disillusion the woman who had obviously been told a series of believable lies to comfort her.

'They said they had finally saved enough to go straight,' Rachel said in a near-croak. Joe watched her eyes, seeing a hint of doubt behind them. Again he said nothing to dissuade the old woman. Instead he stood and asked:

'Where's the money?'

'The what? I don't understand you.'

'Of course you do. It's in a green metal box.'

'If I don't tell you, do you mean to kill me?' Rachel asked. She looked older with each passing minute.

'I try not to make a habit of killing people,' Joe answered. 'It's just that that money belongs to someone else. I intend to take it back to her.'

'I was afraid of that,' Rachel said in a trembling voice. 'I guess I knew. It's on the top shelf of the kitchen cupboards, on the right side. Trace put it up there before they left for town.'

'Would you like another sip of water?' Joe asked. Rachel's eyes were closed. Her head rocked from side to side.

'No; just do what you must and leave me alone, will you?'

Despite indications that the woman was exhausted and unaware of what was actually happening, Joe kept his eye on her as he walked into the kitchen searching for the strongbox. After all, she had tried to brain him with that poker. Fortunately, it seemed that Trace Banner was no taller than Joe himself, for by opening the cupboard door and running his hand along the shelf, he was able to find the box.

Pulling it down, he opened the green box again. Most of the money was still there. It seemed to him that five or six of the twenty-dollar gold pieces that had been in the small wooden rack were now missing, however. Money to be spent on a horse and carriage in Flagstaff, he guessed.

Joe walked back into the living room, the box under his arm. Rachel lay with her eyes closed, the wrist of her right hand over her face. Joe sighed and asked:

'Will you be all right, ma'am?'

'As soon as you leave, I'll be fine,' she said in a particularly bitter voice.

Joe wondered if Marcie and Trace had not promised the old woman a share of the money to comfort her in her later years. It didn't matter now – he was still going to return the cash to Tess Malloy. That was all he cared about. Whatever machinations they had been up to did not matter a bit to him.

He stepped out into the sun-bright yard. Fine dust blew across him beyond the twin pines standing there. It was being stirred up by the four-wheeled carriage being briskly drawn by matched bay horses approaching the house.

EIGHT

Trace Banner was not a happy man. Marcie Malloy was in a fury. She had recognized Joe Sample from a distance. Trace Banner, scowling, drove the covered buggy as if he were a messenger from hell. Joe Sample had not seen the grim-faced, dark-eyed Trace Banner before, but the look he got from Banner as the man pulled the carriage to a stop was one he might have gotten from a life-long, hated enemy.

It was the strongbox under Joe's arm, of course, that had triggered this dark rage.

Marcie leaped from the carriage before it had even halted, her small blue hat twisted to one side. She was a writhing, cursing, stuttering dervish as she reached toward Joe, trying to tear the shallow green box from his grasp.

'It's mine!' she continued to scream as Banner slowly knotted the reins of the two-horse buggy

106

around the brake lever and stepped down, his manner cool, his eyes like coal fire.

'No, it isn't,' Joe said with a calm patience which infuriated the little blue-eyed doll even more. 'I'm taking it back where it belongs.' He noticed, glancing back, that Rachel had appeared on the front porch, her hands empty, her own eyes ablaze. 'I don't think you're going anywhere,' Trace Banner said with quiet menace. He had his pistol in his hand, and the hammer was already drawn back.

'Afraid so,' Joe said with more confidence than he felt. The mock bravado was probably useless – Trace Banner didn't seem to be the sort who would back down.

'Why?' Banner asked, seeming genuinely puzzled.

'I made my promise to Pierce Malloy,' Joe said. In Joe's mind that settled everything.

It did not, however, to Banner or to Marcie who shrieked 'Pierce is dead! You told me that yourself.'

'Obligations can live on after death,' Joe said. Trace Banner laughed.

'What kind of crazy are you? Dead men don't come back haunting.'

'Not exactly,' Joe began to explain as the dry wind washed over them and Rachel stood on the porch, her hands clenching and unclenching. 'But it is—' Joe never got to the end of his sentence. He was interrupted by Trace Banner who lifted his pistol and snarled:

'I'm tired of listening to your foolishness.'

As Banner triggered off, Joe turned away and snatched at his own holstered pistol. Banner's shot sang off the metal box, twisting it from Joe's hand. Joe flung himself to one side against the dry earth, firing twice as he fell. Both shots missed Banner who took two steps forward, raised his pistol and instructed Marcie, 'Grab the strongbox, girl,' and then turned his sights again toward Joe.

'You, cowboy . . .' Banner said disparagingly, but he was talking too much, achieving too little. A man who lived by the gun should have known better. Joe rolled away and fired two hasty shots from his back. One was a near-miss, the second caught Trace Banner in the abdomen.

Gut-shot, Banner grabbed at his belly with his gun hand, folding over, sudden fear in his black eyes. Joe, seated against the earth, shot him again with deliberate aim, and Banner took a spinning .44 slug in his heart, jolting him backwards.

Rachel cried out some shrill curse; Marcie began screaming again. Banner lay still on the earth. Joe rose slowly and snatched up the green strongbox Marcie had been reaching for. There was a bullet-caused groove in it now. Marcie looked at him with her blue eyes misted and then darted toward the body of the gunman. She collapsed over him, sobbing. Joe couldn't tell if it was the loss of Trace or the money she was mourning. Rachel had become a mummy. The old lady hesitated and then silently hobbled from the porch into the shelter of her home.

Both women had lost their hopes for the future within a matter of seconds.

Joe did not feel guilty, although events had shaken him. He stumbled toward his black horse, his leg again throbbing as a result of his sudden movements. Stuffing the cash box angrily into his saddle-bags, he swung aboard heavily and turned the black horse's head with a sharp jerk of the reins. Offended, the horse tossed its head, then settled and started along the lane toward the road to Flagstaff.

The dry wind blew, lifting dust into Joe's eyes. He was angry, tired and disgusted with himself and everyone else. He had had just about enough of this trek. If some ragged woman with a couple of orphans at her side would have approached him just then and asked for a few cents, Joe would have given her the entire fortune and ridden away. There were no orphans passing by, however.

Tess Malloy was waiting for him, he knew. He wondered if the outlaw gang had returned from their excursion, wherever they had been, and if they would be grateful to Joe or in a mood to cause trouble.

Halfway to the road Joe saw three men on lath-ered horses approaching him through a veil of dust. He had never seen them before, but he knew them on sight. Who else would be riding so hard to find the thieving Marcie? Who else would know where she could be found? Joe slowed his horse and watched as Cornish, Stiles and Frank Singleton whipped their ponies toward him.

He thought briefly of trying to flee. His horse was fresh; theirs looked worn to the nub. But the black could not outrun a bullet. Besides, he decided, he had done nothing to these men, outlaws though they might be, they wouldn't shoot him down for nothing – or would they? He drew his horse to the side of the lane and waited.

These last members of the Malloy gang halted before him in a swirl of dust. Their horses shud-dered, the men were breathing hard, their faces glossed with sweat. They each wore dusters, but the long coats, open, did little to conceal the small arsenal of weapons each man was carrying. Not a one of them carried less than two revolvers, and Joe could make out the hilt of a stag-handled bowie knife riding on the belt of their leader.

He was lanky, wore a thin mustache and had large, somehow brutal looking hands. His reddish hat was tugged low to shield suspicious eyes from the glare of the sun.

'Thought you might have been someone else,'

110

this man said, The two flanking him were both angry looking, solidly built men. Their horses bowed their head in weariness. They had been ridden long and hard. Presumably Tess had told the men where she believed Marcie and Banner could be found, as she had told Joe.

One of the flanking riders asked roughly, 'Do you know Trace Banner?'

'Not to shake hands with,' Joe answered.

'But you seen him, right? Up at the house?'

'I saw him.' Joe saw no point in denying it. 'He's dead.'

'Is he?' Their leader, whom Joe took to be Frank Singleton, asked with suspicion.

'Yes. Shot dead,' Joe explained.

'Who did it?' Singleton demanded.

'I did. I didn't like his manner,' Joe said. 'That is, he was trying to kill me.'

'I see,' Singleton said, rubbing his chin, Joe watched their hands warily, not knowing their mood. 'Was Marcie with him?'

'Marcie?' Joe asked blankly.

'His woman,' the second man said. 'Little blue-eyed doll.'

'She's still with him.' Joe admitted.

'I see . . .' Singleton said. Then coldly he asked, 'What's your name, stranger?'

'Joe Sample,' Joe said, growing uneasy.

'He's the one!' the second man shouted,

111

making a move toward his gun.

'Shut up and sit still, Cornish,' Singleton ordered. 'I'll take care of this. You are the one, then,' he said to Joe. 'The one that was sent up here, determined to retrieve the money for Tess?'

'Yes,' Joe said simply. The two men beside Singleton both began to snicker for some reason.

'Quit it Cornish, Stiles,' Singleton said. 'Where's the money, Joe Sample?'

'I don't know,' Joe lied. 'Look, I met Pierce Malloy the day he was killed in Yuma. I made him a promise that I would try to get the money to Tess. I think I've done about all I could to keep that promise. You'd better ask Marcie where it is. I'm done with the whole thing.'

'He's got it,' the man named Stiles said. Cornish added:

'He rode all this way to have it out with Trace, killed him, and then just gave it up? Don't sound right to me.'

'Nor to me,' Singleton said, slipping a Colt revolver from his holster. 'We'd better have a look in those saddle-bags of yours, Joe.'

'Look,' Joe responded without raising his hands. 'Wherever that money is, it belongs to Tess Malloy, right? That's all I care about, getting it to her. Her alone. Pierce promised his brother, Amos, that he would do that, and I promised Pierce. You boys rode with Pierce and Amos, shouldn't Pierce's last request be honored?'

'Sure,' Singleton said, cradling his Colt in his curled hand.

'Ah, tell him, Frank,' Cornish pled.

'The girl you met – the redhead with a patch of freckles? – that's Patsy Graves. She told you the same lie that Marcie had prepared for you. Banner and Marcie tied her up and stuffed her in the closet so that she couldn't give them away. But Patsy figured she had no choice, the boys and me being gone, her not knowing how long we would take to get back. She lied to you just like Marcie did, trying to get her hands on the money.'

'Then where. . . ?' Joe sat the impatient black horse staring at the men facing him, then looking into the distances. What sort of fool's errand had he been sent on? 'Then where is Tess Malloy?' he asked plaintively.

The man named Stiles told him frankly, without expression, 'When Tess got the word along the telegraph wire that Amos was dead, she cut her own throat with a butcher knife. We buried her out back under a pepper tree.'

'It can't be true!' Joe said. Had this all been nothing but a tragic farce?

'It's true,' Singleton said calmly. He still held his gun at the ready. 'Now, if you have no objections, we intend to search your saddle-bags, Joe.'

'All right,' Joe said with apparent resignation.

113

He swung to the side of his horse, but did not let his feet touch the ground. With his left foot still in the stirrup he slapped the black horse on the rump – hard. In surprise the horse bolted forward through the rank of gathered outlaws. One of them loosed a shot at him, but it missed wildly and Joe was in no position to fire back.

Clinging to the pommel, he glanced back and was able to swing into the saddle after a few hundred feet. Looking back, he saw that the Malloy gang was still turning their horses, deciding whether to rush after him or not on their bone-weary mounts.

Eventually they did decide to take up the pursuit, but if their hearts were in it, the flesh of the long-ridden horses was not. Nevertheless, Joe wasted no time in lining his horse away from them. They were only a few miles from Flagstaff, but Joe thought his best chance lay in taking to the rough country surrounding him.

Weaving the black horse through the pine woods he soon came to a craggy gorge where a river flowed freely with a white-water rush. Looking back, he could see the pursuing outlaws. They were gaining no ground on him, but neither did they show any intention of letting up the pursuit.

With the roar of rushing water in his ears, Joe started the black down the canyon edge. It was not his first mistake of the day, but proved to be his last. Joe heard the snap of leg bone, as sharp as the crack of a bullwhip, and the black horse stumbled, staggered and then went down. As Joe kicked free of the stirrups the animal began to slide down the rocky slope, its eyes wild, wide with pain and fear.

Joe half ran, half slid down the hillside after it, but he already knew there was nothing that could be done for the injured animal. Stopping beside its heated, frantic body, Joe did all that he could with regret. He withdrew the cash box from the saddle-bags and positioned his Colt .44 beside the horse's ear. He triggered off and the black horse ceased its thrashing. Joe made for the canyon bottom, his pursuers gaining precious time.

Joe ran, he slipped, he slid toward the bottom of the gorge and its frothing, raging water. He tore his elbow, his knee, twice lost his grip on the green metal box as he sprawled against the rough ground, and continued on. Pausing for breath behind a white-streaked gray granite boulder, he looked upslope and with a tinge of panic saw that the outlaws, far from giving up their quest, were closing ground on him. Their horses, weary, perhaps, but seemingly more sure-footed, far more nimble than Joe's black had been, were making their way steadily down the face of the rocky, pine-studded bluff.

The riders must have seen the black horse by

now; they must have made up their minds that Joe Sample did indeed have the stolen money.

Why did he have it? Joe was no longer sure. He felt like just surrendering the box, throwing it out on to the trail for them to find and keep. Joe didn't want the money, and all it had brought him was misery – yet it belonged to someone else. Perhaps to someone far away who needed it badly: a bank on the verge of collapsing with all of its depositors paying the price; some cattleman who had worked for years to build up his spread, risking all on a long drive to market . . . there were many possibilities. Joe, who had risked all for the sake of the dead woman, Tess Malloy, now decided that he had the same obligation to some unknown entity.

He clutched the green box tightly and raced on as the horsemen made their patient way down the long slope.

The hill slope was slick, mostly shingles of rock and slippery green grass. Below, white water rushed through the channel of the gorge. Joe knew instinctively that he was making a mistake. It is always the high ground that should be taken by a fighting man. But he saw no way up. No way out except into the rush of the river current, and he did not wish to dive into that cold water carrying the strongbox.

The land was flatter now, and he wove his way through the pines standing there, hoping that the pursuing horsemen could not follow quickly. The scent of the trees was heavy, the ground underfoot spongy with fallen needles. He startled a group of crows who had been peacefully hunched among the treetops, and they rose to wing in a black swarm, certainly giving away his direction of travel if it had not previously been known to his followers.

Joe looked around frantically as he came to the river's edge. He was bent over, panting heavily, the useless green box gripped tightly in one hand.

It was either into the river or back up. He ran on a little way downstream, eyeing the frothing current of the creek. He knew he was not going into the water. When he paused, needfully, for breath he found himself at the base of a sheer gray bluff which, at its height, towered even over the tall lodgepole pines. Joe doubted he could scale it, but events were leaving him with few options. As he stood there, looking up the craggy bluff one of his pursuers fired a shot. Much too close, the bullet whined off the rock a foot or two above his head, powdering him with stone dust.

Liking none of this, Joe fashioned a hasty sling out of his scarf, wrapped it around the box and tied the ends to his belt. Then in a near-panic, he began his ascent. His fingers clawed at narrow, weather-formed crevices and his toes scrabbled for any purchase. Looking upstream and below he

117

could now see Singleton and his men emerging from the deep forest. All three had slipped their rifles from their scabbards and now they began firing from horseback.

Joe wondered if he should have tried the raging river which would at least have swept him away from the flying lead – before it tugged him under and drowned him – but he had made his choice and there was nowhere to go but up.

If he could make it up.

His right hand lost purchase as rock crumbled away under his fingertips and he nearly fell. Fortunately the toe of his right boot was wedged tightly into a small crevice and he managed to find a new grip. Two of the crows he had frightened had returned to slowly circle, watching him with yellow eyes. A flurry of shots from below sent them squawking away.

Joe automatically ducked his head, knowing that it was a futile move. He drew his face away from the stone far enough to look up. It was not that far to the rim, and hanging over the edge of the bluff was an exposed pine root. If it were strong enough to support his weight. . . . He would not know until he tried it.

Three more rifle shots, six, pinged off the rock face, ricocheting away into the distance. Joe kept climbing now, frantically, his back, chest and face dripping perspiration. The wind did nothing to cool him, but it toyed with his shirt and trousers as if it might fitfully tug him off of his precarious perch. Joe did not look downward, but he knew he had climbed at least a hundred feet from the river.

His pursuers were nearer, their aim surer now. Joe heard and felt a bullet whine off the rock only inches from his foot. Another just over his head dusted him with powdered rock again. He looked up, saw the tree root within his grasp and lunged for it. His right hand caught a grip, slipped off and fell away in a shower of earth and debris. Frantically he clawed at it again, this time got a firm grip and risked using his left hand as well, as bullets peppered the stone around him.

Joe had to give up the purchase his boots had found in the cracks of the cliff face and attempt to ascend with only the strength of his arms if he were to make it to the rim, to safety. He had left himself no options and so as the bullets continued to fly, he gripped the tree root with both hands and climbed it. Dirt and rocks fell on to his face, but he paid these no mind. Half blind, he struggled up the root, dangling out into space as the bullets continued to follow him up the bluff.

His shoulders ached and his heart was racing with fear. His lungs were burning when a minute, five minutes later – time had lost all meaning – he was able to swing his right leg up and on to the flat ground of the cliff rim. Reluctant to let go of the root, he was encouraged by another group of shots to throw his right hand up as well, and claw for purchase against the rim rock.

Rolling, he was up and over in seconds to lie panting, aching, against the short grass of the rim. After a few minutes he sat up, sucking air into his lungs. Looking around he saw a dozen or so wind-bent pines, a small stand of twisted manzanita and a clump of thorny mesquite, all surrounded by the yellow-green short grass. The wind continued to blow, ruffling all in its passing. Joe could hear the hostile murmur of the creek far below.

He was safe, then. Or was he? He could not tell by the lay of the land which way Flagstaff was situated. He did not know if there was a trail on the back side of the bluff which would allow the horsemen to catch up to him. He untied the scarf from his belt and used it to mop his perspiring face. Looking down at the green box, he considered leaving it where it lay, thought about winging it off the cliff to those below who were so determined to reclaim that which was never theirs.

Joe did neither. Some twisted sense of honor forced him to carry on. He rose unsteadily to his feet and started through the trees in the general direction of Flagstaff, the strong box still held beneath his arm.

NINE

It grew darker, cooler in the pine forest. Joe Sample knew he was not alone on the mountainside. Now and then he heard a horse whicker and at least once what he thought was the voices of men in low conversation. He had a problem.

To simply stroll down the pine-clad hills in the direction of Flagstaff would be a mistake. The men following him would surely know that this was the only destination possible, and although they were not strictly local men, they were from the area, and probably knew the trails and the lay of the land better than he did. Their predations took them far from the home ranch frequently, or so 'Tess', now identified as Patsy Graves, had told him. They must be at least somewhat familiar with the area, whereas Joe had never seen this country before.

He could make it more difficult for them by circling toward town – not in the direction of the river, certainly, but toward the east where the pines grew even more closely together and the land leveled somewhat. They would have to spread out to find him instead of riding in a bunch.

Or so he believed.

He trudged on as the day aged and the cool shadows beneath the pine forest lengthened and grew cooler. He was high enough off the desert that he knew night would settle quickly and bring a harsh chill with it. The wind still blew, rattling its way through the tall timber, dropping an occasional dead branch and multitudes of pine cones along his chosen path. He startled a foraging five-point mule deer buck as he trod on, and later came across a badger which, for a moment, seemed ready to fight for possession of its domain but finally waddled away with an angry hissing sound.

Night would soon be settling, but Joe saw not a single light across the land below where Flagstaff should have been found. And then he did – a brief flaring arc of light – and he froze in his movement, reaching for his holstered Colt revolver.

The light was insignificant, quickly extinguished. It was followed by the wafting scent of tobacco burning. They had found him, or at least one of the three trailing riders had. By skill or chance, it did not matter. He had to get past this man – he had had the briefest glimpse of the big bony roan horse the man in the duster was sitting, and believed the man to be the one called Stiles.

Joe paused, his back against a huge woodpecker-pocked old pine, peering into the near-darkness. The purple shadows allowed him to glimpse no more than he already had seen: Stiles, if that was who it was, leaning with his hands on the pommel, a freshly rolled smoke dripping from his lips.

As silently as possible, Joe placed the strongbox down and crept forward.

He had to take his try at Stiles before the other two could show up. Any shot would bring them on the run, but if he could get Stiles's horse away from him, he had a chance at out-racing Cornish and Frank Singleton to the safety of Flagstaff. Perhaps not a good chance, but a chance. All three of the horses he had seen were worn to a frazzle, and Joe knew he might not be able to get any speed out of the roan.

If there were a way to take the horse without alerting the others with a gunshot ... then that chance was lost: Joe's boot cracked a dry pine twig in passing, and Stiles, who made his living with his own alertness, spun toward Joe, snatching at the pistol hidden beneath the flap of his coat. There was no choice at all. Joe moved to one side and fired up at the horseman at the same time that Stiles fired at him. That one short step to the side might have saved Joe's life, for he was certain that the outlaw was a practiced shot. The bullet from the flaming muzzle of Stiles's gun whipped past Joe's head and slammed into the big pine with a sound like an ax cleaving wood.

Stiles was not so lucky.

Joe's bullet ripped into the bad man's chest, inches below his shoulder and shredded muscle on its way to his heart. Stiles threw his hands into the air, his revolver dropping free, and then fell from the saddle, his cigarette still alight in his mouth. The light from the ember of the cigarette was extinguished as Stiles hit the ground and his startled roan horse danced away and took to its heels. Joe stood looking at the dead man as the horse ran downslope, leaving the scent of dust in the sundown air.

Cursing his luck, Joe checked Stiles for signs of life. Finding none, he rose with his heart pounding, returned to the green box, hefted it and started on. At least, he thought, that was one fewer of them. What good it would do him without a horse, he could not have said. Two mounted riflemen would have every good a chance as three to bring him down, and he knew it. He tried to hurry on, but the light was getting very poor and he did not know the way. Twice he tripped and went sprawling, nearly losing the box in the dusky evening.

He heard horses coming in his direction.

He had expected it, of course, after the shots were fired, but hearing them lifted his already accelerated heart rate to a thundering in his ribcage. In blind panic he continued on. He began weaving through tight copses where the trees grew so closely together that a man on horseback would have difficulty following him. He looked for drop-offs, stony declivities a horse could not maneuver down. In the near darkness over unknown ground it was nearly futile.

Joe Sample halted for breath, doubled over with the strain of exertion. His leg had begun to ache again; he no longer had the speed of his youth. Ahead, now, through the dark ranks of the pines he could see a hint of light, of many lights twinkling like so many fireflies. That was Flagstaff, then, and safety. . . .

If he could make it that far before the killing men behind him ran him down.

Clutching the strongbox tightly to his side, he started on. There was no other choice left to him. By the poor light of scattered stars and the glow of the slowly rising moon, he found a trail – little more than a rabbit run – descending into the darkness of a canyon below. It seemed too narrow for a horse to follow, and so he made up his mind and plunged ahead, following the unknown trail into darkness.

Slipping again, he skidded forward, nearly to

the edge of the steep path, and ended up on his back, falling hard. Lying there, the breath driven from him, he thought again of simply tossing the metal box into the abyss at his right – but what good would that do? His pursuers could not find it in the darkness, would follow until they could confront him. They would decide that he was lying, and do whatever they had in mind. No, there was no point at all in hurling the green box away. It would do nothing to save his skin; would fail to restore the money to whomever it rightly belonged.

Feeling that the blows he had taken to his head along the way had caused him to be more than usually stupid, Joe rose and continued on his way. At one point he realized that the lights of Flagstaff had grown brighter: they no longer flickered as they shimmered through the atmosphere. The town was not far off. If his leg, his heart could hold out for just a little longer. . . .

He heard a cry from above – they had found him.

Despite his conviction that a horseman could not follow that trail, he glanced back to see two shadowy mounted men riding down the steep, winding trail. Joe watched them for a minute in disbelief. They were mad! He knew that he was carrying a small fortune, and that they considered him worse than a thief, a traitor to the gang – illogical though that was. They also knew by now that he had killed Stiles. Rage and greed drove them on. There was no telling which was the master emotion.

Joe heard a clumsy, scrabbling sound, and as he looked toward it, he saw one of the horsemen on a frantically striving horse which, striking its hoofs against slippery stone and failing to find purchase, tumbled toward the canyon depths below, the rider shrieking a curse as both fell, the horse slowly turning in the air, the man cartwheeling toward the rocks below. The second man – Frank Singleton – continued grimly on.

As did Joe. He had reached level ground once more and he raced on as quickly as his badly-healed leg, his lungs and heart would allow him to. He once more entered wooded land, though the trees were more widely spaced. Ahead of him a dark, bulky figure lifted its head to study him as he approached.

It was Stiles' roan horse, standing dismally alone in the forest.

Joe approached with ultimate care, speaking in a low voice, holding out his hand as if offering the animal some treat. The roan had run itself out, that was obvious. It stood shuddering in the dark, watching Joe's approach with wary, starlit eyes.

Amazingly the animal which stood trembling in the night let him approach and put a hand on its bridle, stroking its neck. Perhaps now weary, confused and lost, it welcomed the attention of a human to direct it.

Horses cannot moan, but the sorrel made a low unhappy sound as Joe swung into the saddle. It was hungry, tired and abused. Joe started it through the pines towards Flagstaff. Its walk was not much quicker than his own, but it provided his leg some relief.

From time to time Joe glanced back over his shoulder, expecting to see Frank Singleton charging down on him. But Singleton's horse had to be every bit as weary as the roan. The horse stumbled beneath him and Joe fought to keep its head up, vowing that he would find a place to stable the defeated animal and see that it was cared for – if the roan could even make it that far.

It was not more than an hour later, with the horse dragging its hoofs, that they entered the lower end of Flagstaff. Uptown the night seemed to be alive with the merrymakers. One gunshot sounded from that direction. Here, the town lay dark and still. In front of him now loomed a stable and Joe guided the animal that way. Sensing food, water and other horses, the roan's steps were a little more lively. Joe only then realized that he was riding yet another stolen horse. He hadn't even noticed what brand it was wearing, but the chances were good that Stiles, himself, had not come by it honestly.

When roused, the stablehand came forward sleepily and took a long look at the lathered, heated roan.

'Man,' he said to Joe in a disparaging tone, 'you sure know how to use them up.'

'There wasn't any choice,' Joe replied, removing the saddle-bags from the roan's back as the stableman undid the cinches on the horse's saddle.

Flinging the saddle, aside, the man asked Joe, 'Do you want to stable him or hospitalize him?'

'A little of each,' Joe answered. The man meant no harm, he knew, and obviously cared about horses. 'Just treat him as well as you can.'

The man nodded. Thankfully he did not ask Joe for money before leading the horse away. For Joe had little if any. But stables seldom asked for money in advance. If a man didn't return to pay for his horse, they simply took it over, and even a beat down roan like the one that Joe had been riding was worth more than their feed bill could come to.

Saddle-bags over his shoulder, the side with the green box making the load uneven, Joe stepped out into the night and tried to orient himself. He knew now what he meant to do, but Flagstaff was a large town and he had returned to it from a different direction than he had used before.

Which way?

He figured he could ask anyone he met, but

there were few people at this end of town; all of the revelers were busy on the other side. He trudged along the dusty streets. His leg had begun to stiffen up. It did not hurt as much as it had, but it felt almost useless. Something like a man with a peg leg would feel, Joe imagined. He was lucky, he reflected, that he himself had not ended up with a wooden leg. The doctor in Yuma must have been better than Joe had feared and suspected after all.

For now he felt as if he could not go on. Entering an alley he found a loading dock and pulled himself up on it to rest and recuperate. The place was silent, dark, smelling of damp wood and creosote. A horseman passed by the head of the alley and Joe's head snapped up. But it was not Frank Singleton, who might be on foot himself by now after running his pony into the ground. Besides, no one hunting Joe would think to explore this dark alley.

A door behind Joe creaked open and Joe spun to see a woman in the darkness. She had her arms filled with litter of some kind. In the darkness she did not at first see Joe, and she walked toward a dustbin on the side of the landing and dropped whatever she had been carrying into it. He heard her sigh. It was not a desperate sound, exactly, but one that seemed to carry the weight of human experience with it. Joe squinted into the darkness, staring at her, trying not to make his own presence known.

Young, she seemed. Slender at the waist. She touched her dark hair and looked skyward. By starlight Joe could see her lips move in some silent prayer or invocation. Her dress was dark blue with tiny white tufts worked into it. There was lace at the throat and at her wrists. She wore a tiny pair of red boots.

Joe smiled in the darkness, Why the red boots should amuse him so, he couldn't have said, but they did. A cat in the alley made a sound and the girl jumped, her eyes going toward Joe. Seeing him she called out:

'Hey, you! Be on your way!' In a voice that was meant to be menacing but emerged fearfully from her lips.

'I mean to,' Joe said apologetically. 'As soon as I can manage it.'

'Are you hurt?'

'More beat-up, beat-down and weary. My leg doesn't seem to want to work,' Joe said.

'You are hurt, then,' the woman, the girl said.

'Yes, Miss,' Joe admitted. 'I am hurt, but if you'll let me rest here a little more, I will be on my way.'

She was nearer now. She bent over him and peered down, her eyes wide, her dark hair shifting as she bowed her head. 'You'd better come inside.' she said.

131

'I thought you—'

'You'd better come inside. I take care of all the hungry, injured dogs I come across down here. I suppose I can spare some of my time for a fellow human being.' She paused and asked quite seriously, 'You're not dangerous, are you?'

'Only to myself,' Joe Sample answered.

He heard the little boots click away and the door was opened again, showing a bright rectangle of lamplight. Well, he thought, I may as well. But when he tried to stand up to follow, he found that he could not. Now, frustratingly, his leg had stiffened up on him.

'Here, I'll help you,' the girl said. She tugged and hefted until finally they had him on both feet. She walked him toward the door to the building, Joe moving his legs cautiously, deliberately, the saddle-bags gripped firmly in his hand.

Beyond the door was an almost square shop with a smaller room beyond. The main room contained rack after rack of women's boots and high-button shoes. The racks lined every wall and drew a line down the center of the floor. There was a counter with a clutter of laces, button hooks and tins of saddle leather, bottles of polish and shoe dyes.

The woman led Joe past all of this into the smaller room beyond. There was a desk in there, a wooden two-drawer filing cabinet, midget-sized stove with its black pipe escaping through a round hole in the wall.

'Sit down,' Joe was instructed. 'I don't keep much around here, but I have cheese, bread and some country ham. I can boil some coffee, if you'd like.'

There was no bed, so obviously the girl did not live here. Joe watched as she crouched and placed some wood into the miniature black iron stove, started the fire, placed a pot on the plate then went to the counter beyond to open a breadbox.

'You're a boot salesman,' Joe said as she sliced off a few thick slices of bread. Smiling over her shoulder, she asked:

'How did you guess?'

'But I didn't see any men's boots. By the way, my name is Joe Sample.'

'Pleased to meet you, Joe Sample. I'm Irma Tate.' She removed half a circle of cheese from one of the small cupboards and proceeded to cut a few hearty wedges from it. 'My father,' Irma told him, 'was a cobbler. After he died I had a little money and decided to make a try at selling footwear – everyone has to have shoes, after all.

'My brilliant idea,' she went on, slicing thick slices of ham, 'was to have a little place just for women. So they wouldn't have to go to a boot shop crowded with rough men.'

'Sounds like a good idea,' Joe said from his seat at the small, cluttered desk.

'Maybe it was, maybe it wasn't. My problem was

I couldn't afford a place near the center of town where the ladies usually shop, so I took this place because it was available. I suppose I was over-eager then, because I seem to have bought too much stock. The place almost supports itself,' she said, placing a plate in front of Joe before tending to the coffee, 'but there is little profit.'

The coffee continued to boil. 'So, Joe, tell me – how did you come to be in the position you're in?'

'Do you have the time to listen to a long story?' Joe asked.

'Plenty. I was just going home to try to figure out a cheap way to spend an evening.'

'No one waiting for you?' he asked as she poured him a mug of coffee.

'No one at all.'

Joe looked at her before he began. She was a nicely fashioned woman, of twenty or so, at a guess, with plenty of dark hair now coming loose from its pins here and there. When she smiled it was pleasant if a little weary. Joe made up his mind, nodded and said:

'Well, then, if you want to know, this is what happened . . .' and went on to relate events from the time the steer had crushed his leg in that Yuma holding pen; the Dog Stain Hotel; meeting Pierce Malloy; the events at the chicken ranch; following the map to the hidden treasure trove; the encounter with Solomon and Moses; the visit to the Malloy gang's hideout to search for Tess; the narrow escape over the hills; the deaths of Cornish and Stiles, leaving out only a few unimportant details. Irma, seated across the desk, watched him, her elbow on the desktop, chin cupped in her hand, her eyes bright. When he was through talking, when his rough meal was finished, she shook her head in amazement.

'You still have the money, then?'

'In there,' he nodded toward the saddle-bags he had been lugging around.

'How much is in there?' she asked.

'I only looked in a couple of times. I think about $20,000.'

'You never counted it?'

'What for – it isn't mine.'

The lady shook her head, 'You are a strange man, Joe Sample.'

'People are always telling me that,' Joe answered with a smile.

'What will you do with it now – now that Tess is dead?'

'I was planning on taking it to the courthouse. I know there is a United States marshal in Flagstaff now. I'll simply turn it in and let him try to find out where it came from, who it belongs to.'

'And then?' Irma asked in a softer voice as she rose to clear away the dishes. 'Where are you going afterward?'

'Why, back to Socorro, to the Double Seven. With my leg as it is, I'm in no condition to be a working hand now. But I have to talk to Poetry Givens. He promised me that he would keep me on the payroll until I was healed, so he should owe me a few dollars' back pay. He might even take me on as a yard man,' Joe said doubtfully, 'although he's already got two old men more crippled up than I am working for him doing chores around the ranch.

'The problem now is finding enough money to buy a horse. I suppose I could try all the stables, see if they need someone to rake out the place or cool the ponies that are brought in.'

'Joe,' Irma said seriously, 'that is the lowest work you could find.'

'I don't have much pride.'

'I mean as far as wages! Do you know how long it would take you to save up enough to buy a decent horse and saddle – and eat at the same time? Months!'

'I suppose so,' Joe said miserably. 'I just don't have any other ideas.'

'Maybe someone would lend you a horse,' she suggested. 'Just to get to Socorro and take care of business.'

He shook his head heavily. 'I don't know anyone in Flagstaff.'

Irma returned to the desk and stood looking

down at him. He could smell the woman-scent of her as she took his hand in her own small, dainty hands.

'You know me,' she said.

'I don't see—'

'I have a saddle horse, Joe. I don't ride it often enough for it to even get proper exercise because I don't really go anywhere except from home to the shop and back again. You can borrow it.'

'Socorro is hundreds of miles from here.'

'I know where it is,' she said.

'Why on earth would you trust a stranger with your horse?'

'Joe,' Irma told him, 'anyone honest enough to carry around $20,000 of someone else's money without even counting it, can be trusted not to steal an 8-year-old horse.'

TEN

It was with some confusion that Joe Sample awoke to the sounds of a mockingbird chattering on the windowsill and the smell of coffee and frying bacon drifting on the air. As he lay in a soft bed watching the Arizona sun rising above the pines he could see on the hilltops beyond the window. He yawned and then sat up with a start. Where was he!

He dressed and staggered out of the room which he now saw was a woman's. It contained little gee-gaws and had a collection of powders and perfumes on the dresser. Proceeding into the interior of the small house, he followed his nose to the kitchen. Irma was there, wearing a pink apron, her dark hair piled high on her head.

'Finally,' she said. 'I was just getting ready to wake you up. I made you breakfast and the coffee's on the stove. Now, I've got to get to work. I sent

138

one of the neighbor boys off to the stable to fetch my gray horse. He should be back by the time you've finished eating.'

'This is all very kind of you,' Joe said, meaning it. 'I don't even remember making my way here.'

'You were in pretty bad shape. I had a hard time managing you.'

'I'm sorry,' Joe said. 'Sorry to put you through all this.'

Irma smiled in response, and it was a bright, cheerful smile. 'Don't be. Maybe you can return the favor sometime.'

'I'd like to, but . . . I don't know if I'll ever be back this way, Irma.'

'Oh, yes you will,' Irma said in a sharp tone although her eyes were humorous. 'I'll be wanting that horse back, Joe Sample!'

'As soon as I can get it back to you,' he promised, not knowing when that might be. He would have to first ride down to Socorro, talk to Poetry Givens and wrangle another horse for himself, then lead her horse back here. A long, complicated business, but he had given his word, besides, he had no other way out of Flagstaff.

Irma served him scrambled eggs, thick-sliced bacon and white grits on a platter. 'You can get your own coffee,' she said. She glanced at a little watch pinned to her bodice and removed her apron. 'I've got to be getting to work. I can't chance missing a customer, as few as I get.'

Joe looked at the small woman and said simply, 'Thanks, Irma – for everything.'

'Eat your breakfast before it gets cold.' she instructed him. There was a far away look in her eyes which settled on him for a long minute before he heard her sniff and turn away, walking toward the door, the heels of her little red boots clicking on the flooring.

The boy with the gray horse arrived just after Joe was through eating and rinsing off the plates the best he could, his thoughts oddly fixed on Irma Tate. Why that should have been, he did not know. He had more important things to consider, but the little woman with the bright smile could not be kept from his mind.

On the gray horse, Joe started uptown after inquiring of the boy who had brought the gray which way the courthouse stood. He found the brick building with its elm saplings in front easily and started up the steps with his saddle-bags slung over his shoulder. Entering the long corridor he started toward its head. The office he had seen the United States marshal enter was that way. He read the gilt-painted ledger on the glass door: 'Hugh Donnely, US Marshal,' and entered. Among the polished wood cabinets, gun racks and newly painted white walls, he saw a single man seated behind the desk. It was not the marshal he had seen the other day, but a young, hawk-eyed man wearing a deputy's badge.

'Help you?' the deputy asked, rising.

'I wanted to see the marshal.'

'He's in court this morning – probably won't be back until after noon. Anything I can help you with? I'm Brad Tabor.' Joe introduced himself and the two shook hands. Joe dropped his saddle-bags on to an upholstered chair and removed the green box.

'I want to return this.'

'To who?' the deputy asked eyeing the box.

'That, I do not know. I figured the marshal could poke around, send letters to other lawmen in the territory and find out who has a claim to it.'

By then Tabor had opened the box. He looked at it, whistled softly and asked, 'How much is in here?'

'I never counted it. I'm guessing it's $20,000 or so.' He knew that Trace Banner and Marcie had pilfered some of the money to buy their fancy carriage. 'Enough so that someone will be wanting it back – I would guess a bank lost it in a robbery.'

'But you don't know for sure?' Brad Tabor asked, his hawkish eyes growing more suspicious.

'No, I don't. I only know that the Malloy gang is responsible for taking it.'

'I see,' Tabor said thoughtfully, closing the lid of

the box. 'What are you – a bounty hunter or something?'

'No, sir. It's just something I . . . came across.' Joe found that he hadn't the energy to tell the long tale again right then. 'I wanted to return it.'

Tabor said, 'I've got the key to the safe. I'll lock it in there and let Marshal Donnely take care of it when he gets back. Do you want to wait around and talk to him?'

'I'd rather not,' Joe said honestly. 'All I ever wanted to do was return the money to whoever it belongs to.'

'Well,' Tabor said rising to shake hands again, 'You've done all you came do, Mr Sample. The rest is up to us, it seems.'

'Thanks,' Joe said, picking up his saddle-bags. 'I'm glad to finally have that off my hands, off my mind.'

'And we thank you for being an honest citizen – a lot of men would have just taken off with it.'

And they would not have gotten far, Joe thought, Not with that money. There would always be somebody after it until it was tucked away in a vault somewhere. It had a hex of some kind on it, and other greedy men with guns would continue searching for it.

Frank Singleton, for instance. And what had happened to Frank? Likely his horse had foundered and he had been left on foot to walk to

Flagstaff. No matter: Joe no longer cared. He had Irma's gray horse and he was Socorro-bound, without the burden of the stolen money. As he swung aboard the borrowed horse and headed toward the rising morning sun, his heart felt lighter than it had in a long time. His only destination was one he knew well: the home ranch, the Double Seven.

The horse was easy to ride. Its smooth gait ate up more miles than seemed to have passed. Irma had said that the gray hadn't been exercised much lately, and the animal seemed to be enjoying its escape from the confines of a stable box. Still, Joe was careful not to overuse it.

After a cold night and a hot day on the desert, the country began to become more familiar. One day after, around noon, he drew up in the yard of the Double Seven ranch house. There were three horses at the hitchrail. Joe spotted the shaggy Ike Cavanaugh emerging from the red barn and he rode toward him. Cavanaugh looked up, his eyes not registering recognition. Then he did know who Joe was and he smiled, throwing his arms out.

'Welcome back, you saddle bum,' Cavanaugh said in a growl intended to mask his pleasure. 'About time you got back to work. Imagine laying up in that fancy hotel all this time!'

Joe didn't take the time to disabuse Cavanaugh of the notion. He was happy to see his old friend

143

and told him so before swinging down from the saddle.

As soon as Joe planted his right foot he knew something was wrong. His leg was not getting better, it was worse. Jagged pain shot up it from ankle to hip. He had started riding before he should have – but what choice had he back in Yuma without a dollar to his name? The leg, he knew, would never be the same, not good enough to get back to work. He vaguely regretted having left his cane behind as he led the gray horse into the barn, limping heavily. Ike Cavanaugh watched him with knitted brow and critical eyes.

'Never did mend right? The leg?' he asked, and Joe just shook his head as he removed the saddle from the gray horse.

'That's tough,' Ike said. 'Why'd you bother coming back to the Double Seven, then?'

'Where else would I go? Besides Poetry said he was keeping me on the payroll until I was healed. I was hoping he would let me have a few bucks to buy a horse.'

'If Poetry said he would do it, he will. Never had a finer boss than Poetry Givens.' Ike watched as Joe finished tending to his horse. Then the older man told him, 'That friend of yours is still working here.'

'What friend?' Joe asked.

'You know who I mean – that Tittle Sparks.

Poetry took him on because of your recommenda-
tion.' Ike added in a grumble, 'Though I can't say
he's much as a cowhand.'

'Tittle Sparks?' Joe said hoarsely.

'He says he knows you.'

'He does. But the one and only time I met him
was when he took $200 from me while I was sleep-
ing,' Joe said angrily. Then he asked, 'Where is he
now?'

'Why, he's over in the bunkhouse, or was, last I
knew,' Ike said.

'I think I'd better talk to him.'

'Don't you want to talk to Poetry first?'

'No. This can't wait.'

Ike shrugged using only his eyebrows. 'Let's go,
then.'

Joe was still trail-weary and on top of that his leg
had begun to stiffen again as it always did after
moments of pain, but he was determined. He
made his way clumsily across the dusty yard, Ike in
his wake, past the big house and toward the
bunkhouse beyond. They walked through the
small grove of dusty live oaks and emerged in front
of the bunkhouse. Three loafers sat on the front
porch, pretending to mend harness and braid
riatas as they smoked and exchanged jokes. Joe
knew two of them, and he nodded.

'Is Sparks around?' he asked one of them, and
the man inclined his head toward the bunkhouse

and returned to braiding his riata.

Joe entered the low ceilinged building's shadowed interior with its rows of double bunk beds and spotted Tittle Sparks almost immediately. He was sitting on a lower bunk, cleaning his rifle.

'Stand up,' Joe commanded and Sparks looked up with surprised eyes.

'Joe Samples!'

'It's me, you damned sneak thief,' Joe said. His hands were tightly clenched. 'The desert didn't kill me after all.'

'I guess you want your buckskin horse back,' Sparks said, rising uncertainly. His eyes went beyond Joe as if expecting someone to help him.

'I want the horse, I want my money. Mostly I want to beat you to a pulp for leaving me stranded out there.'

Sparks was cornered. He tried a weak, unconvincing smile and then took the rifle he had been cleaning, gripping it by the barrel, and swung wildly at Joe's head. Joe ducked and it missed, arcing around to strike one of the bunk bed's uprights. Joe launched himself at Sparks. His shoulder caught Sparks in the chest and sent him back on to the bunk, his arms flailing as he tried to fight Joe off. With Joe on top of him, Sparks could hit nothing but Joe's back with his wild punches. Joe grabbed the front of Tittle's shirt and held him up briefly before driving his fist into Sparks's face twice. Groaning,

Sparks went limp, his eyes rolling back in his head. Limp now, he rolled to the floor and remained there. A group of men had gathered around them to watch the fight. Now one of them called out:

'The boss is coming!'

As Joe stood panting, trying to regain both breath and composure, a familiar figure appeared in the doorway. Poetry Givens wore a white shirt and gray linen slacks. His silver hair was neatly barbered, his flourishing silver mustache twitching slightly, blue eyes cold.

'What's this? You men know I won't stand for any fighting on this ranch.' He squinted into the darkness of the bunk house, his eyes still adjusting to the change of light from the brilliance in the yard beyond the doorway.

'Joe? Are you back?' Then he caught sight of Tittle Sparks who had managed to sit up and now sat sagged against the wall.

'This man stole my horse, my money and left me afoot on the desert,' Joe said. He wiped back his hair and walked forward to meet his employer. The two shook hands. Poetry had noticed Joe's limp. 'Never did heal right, huh? Well, Joe, I guess the man had it coming, if what you say is true.'

'How much did he take from you, Joe?' Ike Cavanaugh asked.

'It was a little over $200, most of it in paper money.'

'Why don't we have a look?' Ike suggested and he lifted up the mattress on Tittle Sparks's bunk. Beneath it was a set of saddle-bags. Ike turned them over and announced. 'Initials "J.S." burned in the leather. Mr Givens.'

'Let Joe have them,' Poetry said.

Ike handed the saddle-bags to Joe, who unbuckled one side of them and looked inside. Reaching in he removed a narrow sheaf of bills. A couple of gold twenty dollar pieces lay in the bottom.

'It's mine, all right,' he said. 'A few dollars missing, but what can you expect.'

'You,' Poetry said in his no-nonsense voice, leveling a finger at Tittle Sparks who still sat on the floor, back against the wall. 'Get off my ranch. I will not countenance a thief.' Then Poetry spun on his heel and left the bunkhouse.

Joe stood over Sparks. The man was nearly blubbering. 'Where can I go – I don't even have the buckskin horse now.'

'You're no worse off than you were when I first met you,' Joe reminded him. 'But here,' he said flipping a silver dollar which landed on Sparks's lap where it shined dully. 'A man has to have a little traveling money.'

'Need some help getting up?' Ike Cavanaugh asked, as Joe Sample prepared to mount his buckskin horse.

148

'No – I'm not that far gone yet,' Joe replied with a smile.

'What did Poetry say to you?' Cavanaugh inquired.

'He first paid me two weeks' back pay, which was big of him and then offered me a yard job, although he's already got two men working around the place. I told him that I appreciated the offer, but I had other prospects.'

'Such as?' Cavanaugh asked doubtfully.

Joy swung his leg up and over the buckskin. 'I was thinking about going into the shoe business, Ike.'

'The *what?*'

'It's not a sure thing just yet, but I mean to give it a try. Besides,' he said, 'I've a borrowed horse I promised to return.'

With that Joe Sample nodded and rode out of the Double Seven yard on his buckskin horse, the gray trailing on a tether. Ike Cavanaugh removed his hat, scratched his shaggy head and got back to work.

ELEVEN

Flagstaff dozed in the golden glow of early morning light. Joe Sample was not the only person on the streets, but there were so few other citizens up and about that it was an almost eerie setting with the empty buildings, shuttered windows and unused plankwalks. Two of the saloons Joe passed were open. Apparently men drank at all hours here.

Joe's first stop was at a stable. He did not know if it was the same one that the bay horse had been quartered in before. His buckskin too was a little trail-weary and ready to be groomed and fed. Joe left both horses in the care of the sleepy stablehand and walked the familiar street toward Irma's house.

He wondered exactly what there was to make him feel hopeful or even welcome there. She had taken in one more injured dog; perhaps that was all there was to it. On a whim and a hope he plodded on. There was always the excuse that he had come to tell her that he had returned her horse.

Joe's leg had begun aching along the trail and now as he neared Irma's house it started, as it always did, to stiffen on him. 'I'm a wreck,' Joe muttered to himself as he stopped in the shade of a large cottonwood tree to rub his leg.

There was a row of white picket fences in front of a dozen cottages that all appeared the same. He was wondering now if he could remember which house was Irma's. He did know that she was an early riser, early to work and most of the cottages seemed to still be asleep. The third one along had a thin column of smoke rising from it and a lamp burned behind a window shade. Beyond it, the rising sun had started to turn from red-gold to white. It was going to be a hot day.

Joe stepped almost shyly on to the porch in front of the cottage, feeling like a schoolboy. He barged ahead, rapped on the door and had it opened to him. Irma had a pink wrapper drawn around her. Her hair was not yet fashioned. Her hand held a collection of hair pins. Joe swept his hat off his head.

'Early, aren't you?' Irma asked, but there was a twinkle in her eyes as she scolded him. 'Well, come on in. Go through to the kitchen. You know where

151

it is. Pour yourself some coffee while I try to make myself decent.' Irma looked down at herself and then vanished toward the interior of the house.

'I brought your horse back,' he said to the empty cottage. Receiving no answer, Joe Sample poured a cup of coffee into a blue ceramic mug and sat at the kitchen table. Carefully, he sipped at the strong brew, wondering about his own impulsiveness once again. He probably should not have come here, at least not so early, but it had seemed important. Along the trail all he could think of was seeing her once more, no matter how crazy his ideas were.

She appeared in the doorway while Joe was pouring himself a second cup of coffee. She had brushed her hair to a gloss and pinned it up. She wore a white dress with ruffles at the wrists and a red bow in her dark hair to match . . . Joe looked down, yes, she was wearing her little red boots. He smiled to himself.

'Did I hear you say you brought my horse back?'

'Yes. It's at a place called Conklin's. I didn't know where you had it kept before.'

'It doesn't matter. Conklin's is as good as any, I suppose. I'll drop by after work and see to a long-term arrangement.'

'That's the other thing I wanted to talk to you about,' Joe said hesitantly. 'A long-term arrangement.'

152

'Why, Mr Sample!' she said with mock astonishment. Joe flushed and replied:

'Sit down, if you've got a few minutes, and I'll tell you what I was thinking.'

Irma nodded doubtfully, poured herself a cup of coffee and sat opposite, facing him with her blue eyes alight. 'Go ahead,' she coaxed.

'It's like this. When I talked to you before you said your store wasn't doing that well because of the location.' Irma nodded, listening intently. 'I can see that, and I have to also think that it's partly because you only cater to the female trade.'

'Yes?' Irma said. Her eyes were questioning, partly amused, Joe thought.

'Here's the thing. I came into a little bit of money. Suppose I . . . you . . . we could find two small shops uptown in a better location. Next to each other, with you carrying on business as before while I had a stock of men's boots and shoes? That way we'd have a better location and, say the whole family needed shoes, they wouldn't have to shop all around, they could come to the one place and both men and women shop for boots.' Joe felt his eagerness waning as he looked at Irma's thoughtful face.

'You as a shoe salesman, Joe Sample? It wouldn't suit you for long.'

'Maybe not, probably not, but after it was all set up I could hire a clerk if something more to my

153

liking came along. . . .'

'Are you doing this all for me?' Irma asked.

'Maybe . . . because of you,' Joe replied, his eyes down on his coffee cup.

'You know, they always tell you not to feed strays because they'll keep coming back.'

'You think it's a crazy idea?'

'I think it's a fine idea – for me. I can't see you wearing a town suit and selling boots.'

'Truth is I'm not good for much else just now,' Joe said. 'I've been fooling myself thinking I can go back to being a working cowhand again.' He lifted his eyes and his gaze met hers, 'And, Irma, a man has to do something to make his way in this world. I'm willing to try it if you are.'

'Willing to risk all your money on this, are you?'

'At least then I would have something, wouldn't I?'

Irma shook her head, 'I'll have to think about it, Joe. Right now I've got to think about getting to work.' She patted his hand and rose. Just then there was a knocking at the front door. 'What has made me so popular all of the sudden?' Irma wondered.

She started that way and Joe followed, his hand automatically going to his holstered revolver. He heard a few muttered words from the porch and then Irma re-entered the house followed by a tall man in an ivory colored shirt, well filled at the shoulders. He wore a thin mustache and a US marshal's badge on his vest.

'Mr Sample?' he asked. 'Joe Sample?'

'That's me,' Joe answered, glancing at Irma who shrugged.

Joe had seen the marshal before, at the courthouse. Maybe he had come to try to find out where Joe had gotten the stolen money from. Instead he asked:

'Where's Brad Tabor?'

'Who?' Joe asked blankly.

'My deputy,' Hugh Donnely said with that slightly cold tone lawmen adopt when they're unsure of a situation.

'I'll make some more coffee,' Irma said, scurrying off.

'Let's sit and talk, Marshal,' Joe said. 'As to where your deputy is, I haven't the slightest idea. I've been out of town for a week and I only ever met the man once, in your office.'

'He didn't ride with you, then?' Donnely asked.

'No. Why would he?' Joe asked.

'I was told,' Donnely said, glancing toward the kitchen where Irma was making busy sounds, 'that you went down to the courthouse to try to return some stolen money – you thought it was taken by the Malloy gang.'

'True. I did and handed it over to Deputy Tabor. He locked it up in your office safe.'

155

'He did not!' Donnely said sharply. 'He hasn't been seen for a week. I'm going to have to go out searching for him, though God knows where he is by now. It was suggested that you and he decided to ride out and split up the money.'

'Hugh,' Irma said quietly from the kitchen doorway. 'I told you that makes no sense. A man who has all of the money doesn't change his mind about keeping it all and invite a deputy marshal to be his partner.'

'I know,' Donnely said, rubbing his forehead with the heel of his hand. 'It pains me – Brad was a fairly good deputy. I thought I could trust him to do right.'

'Twenty thousand dollars is a lot of temptation,' Joe said.

'Yes,' Donnely replied. 'Still . . . I have to raise a posse, Sample. I don't suppose you'd be interested in going along.'

Joe resisted the impulse to laugh. He shook his head. 'I'm in no shape for something like that, Marshal.'

'That's right – Irma told me that you have a game leg.' Joe noticed he said 'Irma', referring to her, not 'Miss Tate'. It wasn't surprising that they should know each other. That told Joe where the marshal had gotten his information. But what exactly were the two of them to each other? Was Joe only a stray dog? He didn't wish to believe that,

He needed to know, but now was not the time to ask.

'I suppose Brad is long gone,' the marshal said, standing and putting his hat on again. 'Probably living it up somewhere, quite pleased with himself.'

'I doubt it,' Joe said. 'I don't think that particular money will ever bring happiness to anyone. It carries a lot of darkness and a little blood with it.'

The marshal and Irma both looked at Joe as if he were a little mad. He didn't seem to notice. The money was traveling again, this time carried by Brad Tabor and not by Joe. He somehow doubted that Tabor would have any more luck than he had.

Irma and Hugh Donnely exchanged a few whispered words and then the lawman was gone again. Joe watched Irma as she turned back towards him. Was Donnely the man of her dreams or just a friend?

She put on a serious face. 'I'm late for work, Joe. Lock up when you leave, would you?' She added apologetically, 'I'm sorry if you're angry with me for telling the marshal all about you, but he is my cousin, after all.'

'Irma—'

'I forgot my shop key!' she said, hurrying back toward her bedroom. Joe moved out on to the porch to enjoy the morning, which suddenly seemed brighter and fresher. Through the garden gate came a specter in ragged clothes, whiskered and filthy with travel. It was Frank Singleton.

'Damn you, Sample,' he croaked, reaching shakily for his holstered gun. 'Where is my money!'

'The money isn't yours, and never was, Frank.'

'Where is it? I need it!'

'How'd you find me, Frank?' Joe asked, moving to one side of the door so that he could pull it shut if Irma decided to come out.

'I asked at the stable. The man there recognized that gray horse and told me who it belonged to. Now quit talking, and cough up that money before I blow your head off!'

Joe moved forward until he was standing just above the steps. He was going to have to shoot it out and he knew it. Frank Singleton looked as if he had crawled all the way across the desert to find the green box. His eyes were glazed. His hand trembled, but he growled.

'Never mind,' Singleton said. 'I'll go in the house and find it myself!'

'No you won't,' Joe said warningly.

'The hell you say!' Frank Singleton bellowed.

Joe had been bracing himself for the impact of a bullet when his bum leg buckled beneath him, and he went sliding down the steps on his back as Frank Singleton fired, the bullet whipping past Joe to slam into the cottage's siding. On his back, Joe drew and fired only one shot, but one was all it took this time. Frank Singleton staggered back, clutching his bloody throat with both hands and then collapsed in the gateway to the little cottage.

The door behind Joe thudded open and Irma rushed out. From up the street he saw Marshal Donnely returning on the run, gun in his hand.

Irma lifted Joe's head and placed it on her lap as she sat beside him on the steps. 'Are you shot, Joe?' she asked, gently petting his head. He tried to smile.

'No. That damned leg of mine just gave out again.'

Donnely arrived and surveyed the scene: his cousin sitting on the steps cradling Joe Sample's head; a dead man crumpled on the path. 'Are there any more around?' he asked Joe.

'Just him,' Joe said and the marshal holstered his gun.

'I saw him walking this way and I didn't like the looks of him. Who is he?'

'His name's Frank Singleton,' Joe said, sitting up.

'Frank Singleton who rode with the Malloy gang?'

'That's him,' Joe answered.

Marshal Donnely tilted back his hat and crouched to examine the dead man. 'He's seen better days.'

'So have we all,' Joe said, managing to stand upright and hobble forward. Irma held his hand tightly.

Donnely looked up at Joe. 'There's a $500 reward posted for Singleton, Sample. I saw the shooting, I'll be your witness.'

'I don't know . . .' Joe said, suddenly weary of everything. Irma interrupted him.

'When can we get it?' In response to Joe's curious expression she said, 'Five hundred dollars can buy a lot of boots, Joe.'

Donnely said, 'I'll have somebody bring a wagon over and get rid of him for you. Reward money will probably take two weeks.'

'Thank you, Hugh,' Irma said. Donnely noticed that she still clung to Joe Sample's hand. He tipped his hat to them and strode away.

'Let's get away from this,' Irma said, indicating Frank Singleton's body. 'Come in the house and I'll make you some breakfast. I believe I'll just skip work today. We have too much to talk about.'

They did, and the conversation concerned itself with more than just boots.